Mists and Magic

Magic on the moors, where mist hides the sunlit valleys below and strangers come walking out of another world; ancient magic that can split a horse's hoof and rob an old man of his livelihood; modern magic that brings a wizard dropping in, punctual to the minute, eight floors up in a tower block— Dorothy Edwards brings together stories old and new in this book of folk tales, legends and poems, and makes the experience the very stuff of magic.

Also available in Young Lions

Paddington Abroad *Michael Bond*
Sunshine Island, Moonshine Baby *Clare Cherrington*
Fancy Nancy *Ruth Craft*
Listen with Mother *Dorothy Edwards*
The Magician Who Kept a Pub *Dorothy Edwards*
The Powder Puff Puzzle *Patrcia Reilly Giff*
Swings and Roundabouts *Mick Gowar*
The Reluctant Dragon *Kenneth Grahame*
Dangleboots *Dennis Hamley*
The Celery Stalks at Midnight *James Howe*
The House that Sailed Away *Pat Hutchins*
Vlad the Drac Vampire *Ann Jungman*
The Reversible Giant *Robert Leeson*
Tales of Oliver Pig *Jan van Leeuwen*
Mind Your Own Business *Michael Rosen*
Cat Walk *Mary Stolz*
Pob and Friends ed. *Anne Wood*
The Boy Who Sprouted Antlers
John Yeoman & Quentin Blake

Mists and Magic

Chosen and edited by
DOROTHY EDWARDS

Illustrated by
JILL BENNETT

Young Lions

First published in Great Britain 1983
by Lutterworth Press
First published in Young Lions 1985
Third impression October 1990

Young Lions is an imprint of
the Children's Division, part of
the Collins Publishing Group,
8 Grafton Street, London W1X 3LA

Printed and bound in Great Britain by
William Collins Sons & Co. Ltd, Glasgow

Contents

Acknowledgments

Our thanks are due to:

Raymond Wilson for the poem *Midnight Wood*
Faber & Faber Ltd for *Night Walk* from the novel *The Witches and the Grinnygog* by Dorothy Edwards
The Trustees of the Alfred Noyes Estate for the verses from his poem *The Moon Is Up*
Margaret Gore for the story *Moon Magic*
Irene Holness for the poem *Witch in Retirement* and for the story *Something Rich and Strange*
Kathleen Hersom for the story *Witch at the Well*
Ann Pilling and the Murray Pollinger Literary Agency for the story *The Old Stone Faces*
Angela Pickering for the story *The Mother Stone*
Pat Kremer for the story *Tilly Witch in the Park*
Ruth L. Tongue and Routledge & Kegan Paul Ltd, London, for *The Sea-Morgan's Baby*, *The Travelling Tree*, *The Grig's Red Cap* and *Four Eggs a Penny* from *Forgotten Folk Tales of the English Counties*, edited by Ruth L. Tongue, 1970
Margaret Joy for the story *Something in the Wind*
Pamela Sykes and Bolt & Watson Ltd for the story *Fairy Godmother?*
Marjorie Darke and Deborah Rogers Ltd for the story *Christmas Crackers*
The National Trust and Macmillan London Ltd for the poem *Cuckoo Song* by Rudyard Kipling

Ruth C. Paine for the story *Cuckoo Fair*

Oxford University Press for the extract from *The Diary of a Country Parson* by James Woodforde

Ruth McDonald for the story *Witchcat Watchcat*

Peter Newbolt for the poem *Against Oblivion* by Sir Henry Newbolt

Anne English for the story *The Pirates and the Drowned Bells*

Pauline Hill for the story *Storm Children*

Frank Charles for the story *The Men of Black Tup*

The Bodley Head for the story *Half a Loaf Is Better than No Bread* from *Four-and-Twenty Blackbirds* by Edward Thomas

MIDSUMMER MAGIC

Now it is the time of night,
That the graves, all gaping wide,
Every one lets forth his sprite,
In the churchway paths to glide:
And we fairies, that do run
By the triple Hecate's team
From the presence of the sun,
Following darkness like a dream,
Now are frolic . . .

from *A Midsummer
Night's Dream*

WILLIAM SHAKESPEARE

MIST AND MOONLIGHT

Dark in the wood the shadows stir:
  What do you see?—
Mist and moonlight, star and cloud,
Hunchback shapes that creep and crowd
  From tree to tree.

Dark in the wood a thin wind calls:
  What do you hear?—
Frond and fern and clutching grass
Snigger at you as you pass,
  Whispering fear.

Dark in the wood a river flows:
  What does it hide?—
Otter, water-rat, old tin can,
Bones of fish and bones of a man
  Drift in its tide.

Dark in the wood the owlets shriek:
  What do they cry?—
Choose between the wood and river;
Who comes here is lost forever,
  And must die!

Midnight Wood

RAYMOND WILSON

Night Walk

DOROTHY EDWARDS

Spit-on-my-finger, anything-you-say, this is how I remember it. Clear as new-leathered glass I can see it to this day.

When I was a girl, years back, I was in service at the Old Doctor's. We had a hard time of it in those days; just me and the cook and all the washing included, and the Missus never very well and the children handfuls.

So came a time when I used to say, 'If I don't get out on my own and stretch my legs I'll go mad with the meejums,' and Cook, being a warm-hearted woman and sorry to see me getting so low, would let me off now and again, and cover up for me saying I was abed if anyone asked (though that rarely happened).

So I made many, many late-night walks along the lanes and over the fields, sometimes I took the old stable-dog but oftener I went alone—for in those days it was safer than it is now to roam o' nights. And tired I might have been and cross I surely had been, but those walks, in wet and fine, wind and calm, cheered me and comforted me.

Soon it seemed as if my feet got to know all the paths and byways and could carry me without my mind having to trouble much where I was going. Here there'd be a whiff of honeysuckle—there a fall and splash as a night-swimmer hit the water. Or, on an icy winter's night with the ground ringing under my feet, I'd stop to see the white frost-lace in the moonlight.

Anyway, it was on such a night-walk I saw what I saw. It was damp that night and cold, and the mist lay in those low patches on the fields. That night my mind was as damp as the Doctor's shirts and the sheets hanging up in the outside wash-house.

There was a kind of light of sorts, though. A sort of half-hearted moonlight that flitted through now and again. I can still remember it, and those patches of mist stirring in the fields as if people were hidden in them. I remember how a rabbit scuttled suddenly out of a hedgerow and sent a shaking of drops from the bramble-leaves that fell with a pat-a-pat like the sound of small footsteps.

I remember thinking it, 'Sounds like footsteps'—and as I went along I went on listening for the sound, although the bramble-patch was well behind me. *And I heard it, pat-a-pat behind me still.*

So I stood stock-still in my tracks and heard it plain: pat-a-pat, pat-a-pat, coming quick behind me, and I knew they *were* footsteps. Very small and light like those of a child, pat, pat, pat, along the hard, damp path with a little stumble and trip now and then just as a child will do when it's in a hurry.

'Bother,' I thought. 'Someone's coming. A child. And if it's one of the Doctor's' (for young Master Philip was up to anything, and might have taken a notion to wander) 'I shall be found out and likely sent packing.'

So I lifted up my skirts a bit, and began to hurry. Thud, thud, thud, went my footsteps and pad-pad-pad came the feet behind me—and they were coming faster and harder like the sound of running.

And then, faster yet, and close behind me, and a little

panting voice saying, 'Please, mistress, please, ma'am.'

It wasn't no voice I knew. So I stopped and looked back.

In that sulky moonlight I made out a little child. A little girl. A white, white little face and dark quick eyes under a big, broken-looking hat. A child bundled under a long rough coat and yet trembling with cold.

'Some parents!' I thought to myself. 'Letting that little 'un roam and romp about on a night like this.'

And, 'Please, missus,' says this little voice, 'can I walk alongside of ye? I am scairt of this old mistiness—it looks like little white ghosties the way it stirs and beckons. I'd be glad if you'd let me walk alongside of you, mistress.'

And I remember that her being so small and low-down would be ever and anon passing through the mist and swallowed up, whereas to me it were at the most breast-high.

'What's kept you out this time o' night?' I says, thinking her folk must be a careless lot to allow it.

'I bin to see my old Grannie, my mother's mother,' she says, in a funny old-fashioned *thinking* way, as if she was trying to remember where she *had* been. 'Hers been sick-a-bed, see, and I didn't like to leave her until my auntie Phillie got home. But I didn't know it would be as creepy-cold as this.'

'Well, come on then,' I says, and so we walked along together.

'I specially don't like walking alone tonight, along of the tales my cousins tells me about ghosties, and that old mist looking so beckony,' she says.

'You don't have to believe in things like that,' I tells

her. 'The poor dead people are very glad of their rest, and aren't likely to want to shake theirselves awake to walk about on a cold damp night like this.'

'But they does, they does,' she says as she pattered along aside of me. 'They're dreadful grim, too. With their bony faces and their little sparkly eyes and their sad voices. My poor old grannie was talking about them only tonight, and how they said "Woe, woe," and how they was watching and warning.'

'Your old Gran is having you on,' I said, not being a spooky-minded person myself.

She was quiet for a while, though I noticed she turned her head quickly from side to side like a dog does when it thinks it smells danger. Suddenly a piece of dead wood undid itself from a tree in front of us and slithered to the ground at our feet, and she let out a cry of fright: 'Oh, I don't like it. I want my Mother!'

'You've been giving yourself the Nasties,' I says. 'Here, take a hold of my hand, the sooner we get on, the sooner you'll see your mum.'

So I took her little hand in mine. It was bare and I felt it cold and bony through the wool of my glove. 'That's better,' I says.

'My cousin Job seed the devils last All Souls' Night but one,' the little thing says, though more perky now she was holding my hand.

'Oh dear,' I think, 'what a superstitious lot her family must be.'

'Job ain't a-fear'd of nothing,' she says. 'Him and Farmer's son stayed up that night for a dare and that's how they saw the demons. Our Job told us afterwards and my Uncle George says yes: he'd seen them too—many a misty night—coming over them meadows down there like fiery dragons. With big white flashing eyes that lit up the hedges, and little red twinkly eyes to their bums, and roaring voices and now and then a screech and a stink to them like the hot smell of Hell. That's what my Uncle George said! And Job and Farmer's son seed sommat else too. They seed a fiery chariot lit up like Hell all reddy and full of demons in dreadful hats, all screeching and laughing, and when they saw our boys they stuck out long, long tongues at them. At that terrible sight them boys scritched aloud and ran home sick as dogs to have seen such beastliness!'

'Come on, lovey,' I says. 'Just stop thinking all that rubbish and talk about something pleasant. Let's have a sing-song,' I said.

She was quick to catch on that idea, so we tripped along together, me singing the bits from *The Belle of New York* I remembered from an old gramophone record at home, and her picking up the words and tunes and joining in like a good 'un.

We sang all the way up through the last coppice. When we reached the top of the path where it opens out into the meadow and dips to the main road, she was a bit ahead, pulling me and looking back and singing: 'The fellows all sigh for me, they would all die for me—I am the Belle of New York!'

Beyond and below was the main road, with little St Jude's church off to the right, and a chain of cars and motor-coaches running up from the coast—for there was a feast of char-a-bancs along there in those days summer and autumn alike—with all the treats and outings going on into the winter. We could hear a screeching of brakes at the corner and see the dipping of headlights.

That little thing swung herself round and looked down at them.

A char-a-banc came up, its inside was all cosy with red-shaded lights. Inside too was a happy crowd of people all a-shouting and singing with paper hats and funny noses. They were shrieking with laughter and fooling about. As they went by some of them put those paper squeakers to their mouths and blew out long coloured tongues. Then another one went by, then another. 'A Works Outing,' I says.

But that child was shaking all over. 'Three of them,' she says. 'Full of fire and devils. Oh, did you see their dreadful tongues?'

I clutched her to me, poor little mite. 'You know they're only charas,' I said, 'chairy-bangs.' But she shook and shook.

'You've been giving yourself the horrors,' I said, while she held me like a mad child.

'Look,' I says, 'there's St Jude's church and there's the road, just as it's always been, and there are the motors and the coaches.'

But she wouldn't look. 'But there arna a road there, Missus,' she says. 'And there arna a church. There's only the pond down there and my home and my Uncle George's place and the little orchard. And I won't be able to get home to my mam and my other grannie because those dreadful fiery things are a-coming and a-coming betwixt us!'

Now this is strange:

I wanted to say something comforting, tell her not to be silly and point out enough was enough. I wanted to pet her too, because I felt the miss of my little sister.

So, not knowing what to say, but determined to put the words to her when I did find them, sensible and clear, I turned my eyes back to the road and *it seemed to melt before my eyes.* Those cars and headlights and coaches, that little church built in my grannie's time—everything just melted away.

And what did I see? Clear as clear, a couple of small cottages and a pond reflecting the poor moonlight. I saw a movement of men, a flicker of flame, and then a rush of sudden fire bursting from every window, and I thought I smelled hot smoke.

It was just a moment and then the mist rolled, and it was all blotted out. It rolled again, and there was the road and the traffic as before.

'That's funny,' I says aloud, 'the mist plays tricks. That's all it is, little 'un, tricks,' I said.

'Devils, devils, devils,' she whispered, her poor little head shaking in that old broken hat.

I tried to lead her forward, but she wouldn't budge. She wound her hard little legs round mine and buried her face in my waist. But I wouldn't have it. Somehow I managed to turn her round to look at the road. 'Look,' I said, 'look, ducky, it's only cars and headlights.'

And I loved that poor little frightened mite so much that she took comfort and lifted up her dreadful little face, and I saw it clearly for the first time in the light of the headlamps.

At that very moment I stopped loving her and pitying

her. I just wanted to get away quick. You remember what she'd said about the ghosts as were 'dreadful and grim with their bony faces and their little eyes like sparkly lights'? That's what I saw under that hat-brim.

I pushed her off in disgust. I'm ashamed to say that—but after all, I wasn't so old as I am now. I hadn't seen death and such then. So I shook off her clinging little fingers and I pulled away.

But the funny thing was this:

At the same time, *she* pulled away from *me*. She pushed *me* off. *She* stared at *me*.

'You ain't 'uman,' she cried out. 'You are a ghostie just like they said. You was one of those all the time.'

She just spat it out at me. 'Bony face!' And then she ran past me, into the open meadow—and vanished. As if the whitish mist had risen again and taken her. Only there was no mist on the high ground where we had been standing.

* * *

> When the mist be all about
> Then let no man venture out,
> It will grip you, hale or stout,
> Without doubt,
> For death he is a-walking, a-walking, a-walking,
> For to find his dead,
> And the marish ground do shiver to his tread:
> Lie safe a-bed!

* * *

The Woman of the Mist haunts Exmoor and the Quantock Hills. At first glance she looks like any other old woman gathering sticks for her fire on a chilly winter's evening; but if you turn to speak to her, or to take a closer look, you find yourself gazing at a patch of mist.

* * *

The Moon Is Up

ALFRED NOYES

The moon is up: the stars are bright:
   The wind is fresh and free:
We're out to seek for gold tonight
   Across the silver sea:
The world was growing grey and old:
   Break out the sails again!
We're out to seek a Realm of Gold
   Beyond the Spanish Main.

Beyond the light of far Cathay,
   Beyond all mortal dreams,
Beyond the reach of night and day
   Our Eldorado gleams,
Revealing—as the skies unfold—
   A star without a stain,
The Glory of the Gates of Gold
   Beyond the Spanish Main.

Moon Magic

MARGARET GORE

H. Manuel, Antique Dealer, the sign read. It seemed a musty, dusty old shop to Robert—most of the things in the window looked like a load of junk. The silver fob-watch, which had lain on its faded blue velvet pad for as long as he could remember, might be worth something, but the rusty toasting-fork—who'd want that? Or the dusty vases, or that Chinese-looking tin tray? However, junk or antiques, there was one thing in the window which fascinated Robert. It was the model of an old sailing-ship, with intricate rigging and so many sails you could scarcely count them.

Every afternoon, Robert turned off from the High Street on his way home from school and ran down the steep, narrow lane where the shop stood, Prow Lane. At the bottom of Prow Lane was the sea—you could smell it and feel it as soon as you turned the corner. Robert had a secret fear that, one day, someone would buy the sailing-ship and he would never see it again. This was why he just had to go and look—every single day.

Robert was mad about ships and the sea. He pored for hours over books about ships.

'When I grow up, I shall go to sea,' he announced.

His parents didn't seem very keen, so now he just hugged the thought to himself.

Today, Friday, on his way home from school, he ran as usual down Prow Lane and pressed his nose against Mr

Manuel's window. He breathed a sigh of relief: the sailing-ship was still there. Robert stood and feasted his eyes on the ship. She was three-masted with square rigging fore and aft. Her timbers looked old but still sound. He had longed to know her name ever since he had first set eyes on her: he had peered and squinted through the dusty shop window, but no name was visible: no doubt the paint had worn off years ago.

Robert had been puzzling his head for weeks over finding a name for the ship. He had always fancied she was Spanish—perhaps because the name over the antique shop was Spanish: H. Manuel. He had considered many different names—and rejected them all. It *must* be just right! Then last night, as he lay in bed gazing at the moonlit window, the name had suddenly come into his head.

Now Robert stood gazing reverently at the old ship. He took a deep breath, his lips moved as he said the words: 'I name this ship *The Castilian Princess*. May God bless her and all who sail in her.'

In Robert's imagination, the wind filled the ship's sails; proudly she cut through the greeny-blue water. Then he was on deck, hair and shirt blowing in the wind. *The Castilian Princess*: she was magnificent!

Reluctantly, Robert came back to reality: he must go home. Just as he turned away, his eye was caught by the model of a small boat, like the old tub his cousin had taken him out in last summer. There were even some oars resting criss-cross inside, as if someone were just about to take them up and row away. The little tub was half-hidden by the ship, but Robert was sure it had not been there before today. He would have liked to go into the shop and ask the price, but he was afraid of looking silly: supposing that, too, was an antique! He hovered uncertainly at the doorway. It was dark inside the shop: all he could make out were some ancient-looking pieces of furniture, and a mass of bric-à-brac in an armchair.

'Just like the Scouts jumble sale,' thought Robert.

He could not see anyone inside the shop, but he had the feeling he was being watched. Better go: he was late already. When Robert reached the corner, something made him look back. A man was standing in the doorway of the antique shop, staring after him. So perhaps he *was* being watched! The man was dark-haired, with a small pointed beard, and was foreign-looking, as Robert had always imagined Mr Manuel to be.

That night, when Robert went to bed, he felt a glow of pleasure at the thought of *The Castilian Princess*. Now that he had given her a name, he could feel that they belonged to each other in a special sort of way. He closed his eyes. *The Castilian Princess* dipped bravely into the waves, sails billowing. At a volley of commands from the captain her crew ran up and down the deck, climbed the rigging, shouted across to each other. *The Castilian Princess* struck out across the wide ocean—and in his mind Robert followed her. He fell asleep almost immediately.

Robert awoke to a sharp noise at the window, as if someone had thrown a handful of shingle up at the panes.

'Time to get up,' said a voice. 'The wind's rising.'

Robert got up at once, pulled on jeans and pullover and his canvas shoes, and went quietly downstairs. He unbolted the back door and stepped out into moonlight.

22

He padded down to the harbour: he knew exactly what he had to do. The moon had spread a pathway across the empty harbour, leaving the old custom-house in dark shadow. Beyond the harbour, a little way out, sat *The Castilian Princess*: Robert knew her at once. She was unimaginably beautiful: all black and silver in the moon-light.

'Moon magic,' said a voice within him.

Robert ran down the steps of the harbour: the wooden tub, with its criss-crossed oars, was tied up at the bottom. A sailor sat in the boat, waiting for him. Robert stepped aboard. The tub was filled with sacks and bags of sea-biscuit. Together he and the sailor rowed away from the harbour towards the ship. Robert could hear voices on deck as they approached.

He climbed up the rope-ladder and helped to load the sacks. The crew had been taking on stores for several weeks: this was the very last consignment. Finally the rowboat was hauled aboard and stowed on deck. The ship was ready to sail. There was a volley of orders—and *The Castilian Princess* was under way at last. When Robert's work was done, he curled up, exhausted, in a cramped corner of the rowboat. He fell asleep at once, lulled by the sound of the sea and the creaking of the rigging.

He awoke with a start. The moon was shining full on his face. He could smell burning. Smoke was coming from one of the holds. He stumbled to his feet shouting: 'Fire! Fire!'

The man on watch immediately gave the alarm signal. The fire-party came running. Men appeared at the hatches, bleary-eyed and cursing. There was shouting, the clatter of buckets, the noise of the pumps, the swish of jets from the hoses. But an ominous smell of dry timber smouldering came up from the hold; flames leaped up high into the night.

'We're doomed!' someone cried out.

'Nonsense!' shouted the captain. 'Keep pumping!'

With all hands furiously working, at last the flames died down and the fire was brought under control.

'Thanks be to God!' cried the sailors. Some fell to their knees.

Robert stood trembling but happy. Then the captain himself came on deck—he was the dark-haired, bearded man Robert had seen in the doorway of H. Manuel's shop.

'*The Castilian Princess* is saved,' he said, smiling. 'Thanks to our ship's boy!'

The Castilian Princess! It was the name Robert had chosen!

Dawn was just breaking when Robert awoke again. *The Castilian Princess* continued on her course, but strangely he was not on board: he was on shore, watching the ship as she blew across the pale sky like a beautiful cobweb. But why could *he* not sail with her? Wasn't he the ship's boy? Or was he . . . 'What am I, *who* am I?'

Robert was in his bedroom, sunshine pouring in.

'Time to get up,' called his mother.

Robert went downstairs like someone in a trance. As he entered the kitchen, he heard his parents talking.

'Must have been a bad fire,' said Robert's mother.

'Yes, gutted right out, the postman said,' replied his father.

'What was?' asked Robert.

'Mr Manuel's antique shop in Prow Lane,' explained his mother. 'Oh, I don't suppose you've ever noticed it!'

After breakfast, Robert raced towards Prow Lane. But suddenly he stopped running. What was the point of going to look at the charred remains of H. Manuel's shop? *The Castilian Princess* would not be there.

With his own eyes he had seen her sail away. Moon magic had made her his for ever.

'The Moon It Is Red'

BEN JONSON

This charm is taken from The Masque of Queens, *a play written over 350 years ago. It was staged for the first time on February 2nd 1608, in front of King James I, his Queen and all the Court, at the palace in London. When the curtains were opened, the audience saw a dark cavern, glowing with fire and wreathed in smoke. Out of the darkness came a troop of witches, calling to the creatures of the night (a 'cat-a-mountain' was a wild cat) and dancing to the music of tambourines ('timbrels') as they wove their spell. February 2nd is the Christian festival of Candlemas, marking the end of the forty days of Christmas; but it was also the first of the year's four great witch festivals, and the audience, knowing this, shivered for fear that the spell might truly work and a blazing storm break over the palace:*

The owl is abroad,
The bat and the toad,
And so is the cat-a-mountain,
The ant and the mole
Sit both in a hole,
And the frog peeps out o' the fountain;
The dogs they do bay,
And the timbrels play,
The spindle is now a-turning,
The moon it is red,
And the stars are fled,
But all the sky is a-burning.

Dame, dame! the watch is set.
Quickly come, we all are met.
From the lakes and from the fens,
From the rocks and from the dens,
From the woods and from the caves,
From the churchyards, from the graves,
From the dungeon, from the tree
That they die on, here are we!

Witches' Charm
BEN JONSON

Witch at Home

DOROTHY EDWARDS

'Several of the inhabitants of these parts are the descendants of witches,' said the woman in grey, waving her hand in a generous sweep that embraced all the valleys and little streams lying at our feet.

She was not at all the sort of person one expected to find upon a mountain summit on a hot afternoon. Clad in a neat suit with a black hat and handbag, and wearing medium-heeled shoes, she had the appearance of a respectable servant of the confidential sort—a lady's maid or companion.

I had set off to climb the steep mountain path that morning. It was a hot day, and I was glad to reach the top. The woman was already there, sitting neatly on a slab of rock. I sat down beside her to get my breath back and enjoy the cool mountain breeze. We fell to discussing the peak on which we were sitting. 'Malkin's Ridge' it was called. The woman told me 'Malkin' was a traditional name for a witch, and that the mountain had been a favourite haunt of witches in olden times.

'Of course, there are drawbacks to having witches in the family,' said the woman. 'Take us, for instance. My Granny was a witch and *her* Granny before her. Indeed, I heard that Great-Great-Great-Granny's Granny was burned by order of the magistrates of her day. My Granny had a pretty bad time with the villagers herself. They

28

pulled down her cottage and threw her into the duckpond which was fortunately not very full at the time.

'But that was in Queen Victoria's time, that was, and what with all the new steam engines and the electric telegraphs, by then the magistrates had given up believing in witches, so half the village was sent to prison and the other half was fined.

'The Squire's lady wife got up a subscription among the local gentry for Granny. They settled her down in a nice new little cottage with lace curtains and everything, and basins of hot soup every day, and free coals and potatoes.

'It was all clean and new to begin with, but Gran soon made herself at home. Once she had encouraged a few spiders and been out on one or two midnight trips round the local graveyards, it looked quite home-like. In fact, in six months you couldn't tell the lace curtains from the cobwebs.

'Mind you, Squire's Lady wasn't pleased. But when Gran made her up a bottle of special medicine that cured her rheumatism, she wouldn't hear a word against her. In fact, she grew quite proud of Granny—said she was "quaint" and used to bring her friends round to watch while Granny made her brews.

'Now, my Gran was very respected in witch-circles. There was always a special place reserved for her at the Sabbat meetings. She had a lot to say in the running of the coven—in fact, you could say she was a sort of chairman of their committee.

'But alas, my Mum was her only child, and she turned out a real disappointment. She just didn't show any

29

interest in the witch profession at all. She hadn't the head for it, I suppose!

'Even a simple little thing like turning herself into a hare went wrong so that she couldn't get back to normal in time for school next day, and my poor Granny had to keep her in a hutch beside the back door telling goodness knows what lies to school inspectors until the spell wore off of its own accord—it hadn't been a strong one, fortunately! The only time Mum ever mounted a broomstick she fell off and went right through the Vicar's conservatory roof! As Granny said, the only use my mother had for a broomstick was for sweeping floors!

'Mad about housework was my Mum. No one knew where she got it from, but there it was. I remember Granny saying that as a baby she'd sit up in her crib and rub away at its wickerwork with the corner of her little blanket for all the world as if she were cleaning it—before she'd grown a tooth to her head!

'Poor Granny did her best, of course. She even engaged a very expensive continental warlock to tutor Mum in the Secret Arts, and she set her up with a fine black cat whose ancestry stretched back to ancient Egypt. But the warlock admitted after only one day's teaching that Mum's was a hopeless case, and was so sorry for Granny that he refused to take a penny of his fee. As for the black cat, after sharpening its claws once or twice on the hearth rug and getting scolded for it by my Mum who couldn't bear the rasping noise, it just got up and walked out of the house, and was never seen again.

'The final blow fell when Mum was eighteen or so. Poor old Granny flew home one night after a particularly successful weekend rally of the Northumberland Malkins to find that her bundles of herbs, her charms, the stuffed alligator and all her bottles of potions had been thrown out onto the rubbish heap.

'In her absence, Mum had given in to temptation and spring-cleaned the house! The windows were shining, the lace curtains had been resurrected, washed and starched and now hung in all their glory with a couple of red geraniums in pots on the window-sill between them, and instead of spiders there was a nice yellow canary bird in a cage singing away happily.

'Granny saw then that she must accept the inevitable. She must just get Mother out of the place. She would have to look around for some nice young man to take her off her hands.

'What my Mum needed was a good husband and a cottage of her own where she could clean and polish and brew and bake to her heart's content.

'Mind you, it was a bitter blow to the family pride and Gran said she sobbed aloud as she carted all her little bits and pieces back indoors. And, as you know, witches are unable to shed tears so it was quite a painful experience for the dear old soul.

'It wasn't easy to find a young man willing to take my mother on—even though she was pretty as a picture and as good as gold—for although the Law mightn't consider our Gran a witch, the villagers weren't taking any chances, and the young men kept away.

'At last Granny had to resort to love-charms. And with Mother grumbling all the time about the smells and the mess on the clean kitchen floor, Granny brewed enough love-potion to start off a hundred weddings. It was so strong that the barest whiff drifting across the village roofs below was enough. In no time at all there wasn't a young man left in the village. They were all clustered around Granny's cottage sighing and moaning and carrying on all night, until Mother couldn't get any sleep for the noise outside, and threw buckets of water out of the window over them—and even then they only went home to change and were back again by cockcrow!

'Naturally the village women were furious, and no one had so much as a nod for my poor mother. If they hadn't been afraid of what my Granny might have done to them, I think they would have done Mum an injury. As it was they sent her to Coventry. She tried to explain that she didn't fancy any of their young men—she said it made her feel silly to have them goggling at her and following her around the village every time she went for a stroll. She asked how they would like it if, every time they went out to shake a mat, they stood the chance of tripping over an exhausted suitor on the doorstep. But it was no use. No one was any the more pleased with her for saying that she didn't fancy one of their lads! Such is the contrariness of human nature. So she was lonely, and like all lonely people she threw herself into her work, and as that meant housework poor Granny had a very uncomfortable time of it.

'I really don't know what Gran might have attempted next, but as it happened, things sorted themselves out very tidily. One day they were having high words about Mother having red-polished the flags of the cottage path, when Squire's Lady, new home from abroad, happened to look in for a chat. The good lady was amazed at the change in the appearance of the cottage, and at the reason for the family discord. She shook her head reprovingly at Granny and said she was to be congratulated upon having such a paragon of a child. "Why," said My Lady, "I haven't a servant in my establishment to compare with her. What a pity you cannot spare her, for I should dearly love to take her into my household."

'This was just the opportunity Granny needed! It took her some time to convince Squire's Lady that she really wouldn't stand in her own girl's light when it came to getting a grand job in a great house, but as soon as My Lady saw that Gran was in earnest, she said she would take Mother into her service at once. "But," she said kindly, "I will send her back to you on one day a week so that she can give the place a tidy-up for you." And Gran was glad to see Mum go—even at the price of having to endure a weekly clean-out.

'When Mother got inside the Big House and saw all those rooms and corridors to clean she was delighted and set to at once to give the place a real going-over.

'After that Mum never looked back. She was in her rightful sphere. She learned to cook and darn and knit, and in due course she rose to be Housekeeper to the Squire. It was then that she married my father who was Head Butler, and they stayed at the Big House until My Lady died. Then, feeling they would like a change, they decided to take on man-and-wife jobs in some of those luxury flats, and did very well indeed out of film people and rich foreigners.

'As for me, well, they got me a job in good service as

soon as I left school. And I've stayed there ever since. Of course,' said the woman in grey, 'times aren't what they were.

'Yes it was funny about my Mum,' she went on, after pausing a moment to reflect, 'but Granny always said that she suspected there must have been some respectable blood in the family somewhere. There had been tales of a Second Footman, a sober young fellow, who got caught in a magic ring several generations back. It's funny how misfits happen in families!'

Finding that she had no more to say, and being now completely rested, I said, 'Well, I'll have to be going if I'm to get any tea down below.'

'Me too,' said the woman, jerking out of her reverie. 'My Lady wants me to babysit while she and His Lordship have an evening out.' She looked at her watch. 'Goodness, I must fly,' she said.

With this, she rose to her feet. After brushing herself carefully down she reached round to the other side of the boulder on which we had been sitting, took up a broomstick which I swear I hadn't noticed until that moment and, mounting it nimbly, was soon skimming briskly downwards through the warm air.

Witch in Retirement

IRENE HOLNESS

Without,
Dead ghost leaves tap
Their feeble, futile hands
Upon the ice-laced pane:

Whining,
The wind searches
Each crevice for entry,
Seeking stillness again:

Weeping,
Rain rivulets
Streak the sea-deep darkness
To hail's insistent drum!

Within,
Dim firelight warmth,
Broom at rest, cat purring:
She hears—but will not come.

Witch at the Well

KATHLEEN HERSOM

There was once a greedy miser-woman called Meg of Meldon.

She was the widow of Sir William Fenwick of Hartington Hall; her father had been a money-lender in Newcastle-upon-Tyne; and she cared for nothing else all her life, but money and money-bags. She never spent a penny if she could help it, she just wanted to get money and keep it.

So she spent all her time growing wheat, and grinding it at her mill, and selling the good sweet flour; seeking gold, and yet more gold. When the harvest was a bad one, she sold the flour back to her poor thin tenants, for a good fat price.

Meg had a crooked nose, and penetrating eyes that stared right through you, and she wore a shabby black cloak and a high pointed hat; so it is hardly surprising that many people believed her to be a witch—looking the way she did.

As Meg grew older, she began to worry about what would happen to all that money after she was dead. But instead of leaving it in her Will to someone who would make good use of it (or even use it to help the poor and sick), she buried little bags of gold in different places on her land in the hope that no one would ever find it, or have any happiness from it. The biggest hoard of all she stitched into a bullock's hide and dropped to the bottom

36

of an abandoned well where she felt sure it would never be found.

Now, when at last old Meg died, that, unfortunately, was not the end of her. She became a ghost; and the ghost of a witch must surely be more grisly than an ordinary ghost.

For seven years she was condemned to haunt the earth, for seven years more she was to leave the earth in peace; then back to earth again for another seven years; and so on; and that was to be the way of it until all the hidden gold had been found and put to some good and useful purpose.

It was, as you might expect, the places where her gold was hidden that she lingered over most often; trying, even as a spirit, to guard the gold for herself. Above all, she haunted the deep draw-well and frightened away anyone who came near it.

Now, there was a young honest countryman working on the Meldon estate, who had a curious dream. In his dream he met a shadowy stranger who told him that Meg's hoard of gold was hidden in the old draw-well by Meldon Castle and that he must try to raise it on the following night. 'But on no account utter a word,' the stranger whispered, 'or she will hear us and come to the rescue of her gold.'

So the next night, shortly after midnight, off went the young fellow to the draw-well, taking with him a long chain, with grappling irons fixed to one end. And there, sure enough, a stranger was waiting, in an old black hooded cloak.

Then, without either speaking a word, the stranger

37

helped him to wind the chain round the roller. The young man made a loose knot near the free end of the chain, through which he slipped one leg; then he allowed his companion to lower him down into the well, like a bucket. He steadied himself against the side of the wall with his free leg. It was a very long, smelly, uncomfortable journey. The pattern of the links pressed painfully into his leg, and his hands were cold and numb with clinging to the chain in that clammy darkness.

He had no idea how much water there might be at the bottom, or how he would grip hold of the treasure.

At last he could feel water with his toe, and then, fortunately, the bottom of the well, only an inch or two beneath it.

Confidently the young man groped for the heavy load in the bullock's hide. He tethered it firmly to the grappling irons. Then he began to climb the chain, keeping his mouth tightly closed for fear his happiness would explode in a shout of joy or a snatch of song. He watched the little round of sky and stars grow larger as he climbed higher; at last, when he reached the top, there was a hand stretched out to help him.

Gratefully he climbed out on to firm ground, and without a word they began to wind up the heavy load of gold.

Up it creaked, inch by inch, and the young man thought it would never reach the top; but, at last, there it was!

Joyfully he reached out for the bundle and, forgetting the warning in his excitement, he called out, 'Now we have her!'

But alas! he did *not* have her, for as he spoke, so the

hide-bag of gold dropped back into the well, and there at the well-head was the gloating form of Meg of Meldon. The young man took to his heels in terror and never came back to Meldon again.

It is said that although all the other hoards hidden by Meg have been discovered and put to good purpose, the gold in the bullock's hide at the bottom of the well has never been recovered; in which case, Meg of Meldon is still abroad—seven years come, seven years gone. But perhaps some quiet person did recover it, and put it to good purpose, for it is certainly a great deal more than seven years since that old witch, or her ghost, was last seen around Meldon.

SPELLS and CURSES

Could you see the wise woman
Down the lane at midnight,
Looking up to make sure
The moon stood aright;
She cropped the dead nettle,
Blew the oak-coals alight . . .
And the Owl of Cwm Cawlwyd
Came out of her kettle!

from *Dead Nettle*

W. FORCE STEAD

The Old Stone Faces

ANN PILLING

Every day, on his way to school, Joe Parker walked with his mother past the old stone faces.

The Parkers lived in a small flat over the tuck-shop in Holywell Street, where Joe's mum was kept busy all day, selling newspapers and sweets and tobacco to all the people who walked up and down that dark, twisty street, one of the oldest and most mysterious in the whole of Oxford. It is a city full of the most fascinating and curious things, but nothing fascinated Joe Parker more than the old stone faces stuck up above some railings round an ancient yellowy-stone building in Broad Street.

There were seventeen of them, all in a row, and each one was different. Seventeen massive stone heads, with stone hair and stone beards, staring out across the traffic at the students going in and out of Blackwell's bookshop. Some of the faces were sad and bored-looking, others were grumpy. Joe's favourite was old Goggle-Eyes who looked as if he'd just seen a ghost. But though they were all different, the seventeen faces had one thing in common— they all looked extremely miserable, and Joe felt sorry for them.

'Come on, Joe,' his mum said one day when they were rushing to school as usual. 'Staring at those funny old statues again! Do hurry up, or we'll be late.'

'Who put them there, Mum?' Joe asked as they went along. 'What are they for? And why do they look so fed-up?'

Mrs Parker wasn't really listening. Her head was full of the things she had to do when she got back to the sweet-shop. There was the new paper boy to talk to, and the ice-cream people to phone, and the old professor's special tobacco to order from the suppliers.

'There must be *somebody* who could tell me about them, Mum,' Joe was saying. 'Surely *somebody* must know.'

It was his mother's turn to stop in the middle of the street. She'd had an idea.

'There is, Joe. I've just thought of the very person. Why don't you ask Professor Owen Morgan Jones? He's sure to know. They say he's the oldest professor in Oxford. He'll be in to collect his special tobacco on Friday. You could ask him then.'

'I *will*,' said Joe.

But when Friday came the rain was pouring down, and Holywell Street was as black as night.

'Joe,' Mrs Parker said. 'Put your anorak on, will you, and pop down to Number Thirty with Professor Jones's tobacco.'

Two minutes later Joe was knocking on the professor's door.

'Come in, Joe,' said a whispery old Welsh voice. 'Come in and get warm, it's a nasty old day.'

Soon Joe was sitting by a roaring fire with a mug of hot cocoa and some ginger biscuits.

'My mum sent you the special tobacco,' he said. 'And . . . and . . .' Then he stopped. He felt rather frightened of Professor Owen Morgan Jones. There was something mysterious about him. His small sharp eyes were such a bright green, and his beard was the whitest and bushiest

Joe had ever seen. He looked centuries old.

'You've got something to ask me, haven't you?' the Professor said, opening the tobacco and filling his pipe.

'How do you know?' Joe asked in surprise.

The old man laughed. 'You don't live as long as I have, Joe, if you don't keep your wits about you, and your ears open. I'm the oldest professor in Oxford, you know. Well, what's your question?'

'It's about those statues in Broad Street, the big stone heads on top of the railings. What are they there for? And why do they look so unhappy?'

Professor Owen Morgan Jones puffed on his pipe.

'People have argued about those heads for years and years, Joe, and none of them knows the true story. Some say they're great Roman emperors, or old Greek poets. Others say they might be advertisements for various kinds of beard—you'll have noticed that all their beards are different, I suppose?'

'I have,' Joe said. 'But that doesn't explain why they all look so miserable.'

Suddenly the professor clutched at his sleeve in excitement. '*That*,' he cried, 'is the most important question of all! Clever boy to have asked such a question! The fact is, Joe, that those stone heads are not kings or poets or advertisements at all. Those are the heads of nothing less than the *Pontybodkin Male Voice Choir*.'

'The *what*?' Joe said.

'The Pontybodkin Male Voice Choir!' Professor Jones repeated. 'One of the most wonderful choirs in Wales. Many years ago they came here and gave a special concert at the Town Hall. It was a marvellous concert, Joe, the whole of Oxford came to listen to them, the tickets were sold out months ahead. But when it was over, and they were going back to Pontybodkin, something terrible happened.'

'What?' Joe whispered.

'A spell was cast upon them, by the Witches of Wellington Square.'

When he heard this Joe nearly jumped out of his skin. 'Are there really witches in Wellington Square?' he stammered. 'That's the way I go to school. We walk through there every day, me and my mum.'

Professor Jones took his hand and squeezed it.

'It's all right, Joe, they left Oxford years ago.'

'Why?'

'Well, nobody liked them very much, and *they* didn't like the climate. They complained that it was too foggy and damp. So they emigrated. But the night of the concert —you do know that witches can't sing, I suppose?'

'No I didn't,' Joe said.

'Well, they can't. Anyway, on the night of the concert they sat outside the Town Hall, blocking the pavement with their broomsticks, howling jealously in chorus while the glorious singing was going on inside. Nobody listened to them, of course, and a policeman moved them on in the end. But what do you think they did?'

Joe shook his head.

'They glided off down the Banbury Road and hid themselves in some big trees, waiting for the Pontybodkin Male Voice Choir to drive past on its way home. It was a cold rainy night, very like this one, and the coach driver didn't look back till he was well on the road to Wales. But after a few miles he turned round and said, "Well, lads, it was a right royal performance tonight. How about a few songs for me?" And do you know what, Joe? That coach was completely empty and all that was left of the Pontybodkin Male Voice Choir was a row of stone heads in Broad Street.'

There was silence in the small, dark room, and Joe listened to the rain clattering against the window. Professor Owen Morgan Jones stared into the fire sadly.

'Such singing, Joe. So beautiful. It would almost break your heart. I should like to hear it just once more, before I die. Will you help me?'

Without waiting for Joe's answer the old man had climbed onto a stool and was lifting an enormous book down from a shelf. He spread it open on his knees and began to look through it. At last he stopped, and read down a page carefully.

'Here it is, Joe. Here we have it. This tells us how to—'

'To bring back the Pontybodkin Male Voice Choir?' Joe interrupted in excitement.

'Not quite, Joe. You see, they've been up on those railings a bit too long really, and when the Witches of Wellington Square emigrated they crossed the sea—and that always strengthens their kind of magic. But at least this book tells us how to make the heads sing again. I'll need your help though.'

'But, Professor Jones,' Joe said, 'why don't you make them sing yourself?'

'I'm too old, Joe,' he said wistfully. 'The book says that what must be done can only be done by a small boy, someone about your age. How old are you?'

45

'Seven and a half,' Joe said nervously.

'That's perfect then. Will you do it?'

'Well, I'll have a go,' said Joe.

A few minutes later it was all arranged. Professor Jones copied something down from the old book, folded the piece of paper, and pushed it into Joe's hand.

'Take it home, Joe, keep it safe. Don't read it yet, but when the time comes, take it with you.'

'But how will I know *when* the time has come?' Joe asked, feeling rather bewildered.

'To release the Pontybodkin Male Voice Choir,' Professor Jones said triumphantly, 'three things are required: a clear moonlit night, a pure black cat, and the words you've just put into your pocket. A moonlit night's no problem, though we may have to wait a bit. You've not got a pure black cat I suppose?'

'I'm afraid not,' Joe said.

'Don't worry. One'll turn up eventually, it always does. Now off you go. Your mother'll be wondering what's happened to you.'

The squally weather lasted for ages. Joe didn't bother to check on the clear moonlit night because he knew there must be thick clouds all over the sky, and in any case the pure black cat hadn't shown up yet.

There were hundreds of cats in Oxford, tabby and tawny, marmalade and grey, black cats with white paws, white cats with black paws, cats that slipped out from alley-ways and rubbed against his legs, cats that peered down at him from crumbling old walls. Once, in the pet shop, Joe thought they'd found the cat they needed, but when it was lifted out of the window he spotted three white hairs under its chin, and he turned away in disappointment.

'I'm sorry,' he said to the lady. 'But you see, it has to be pure black.'

Then, one night, when he was asleep, bright moonlight shone into his eyes and woke him up. He got out of bed and tiptoed across to the window to look out. The night was thick with stars, and the most brilliant moon Joe had ever seen was floating across the sky. *It was time.*

Quickly he felt under his mattress for Professor Jones's piece of paper. Then he crept downstairs, through the shop, and stepped outside into the cold crisp night.

Seconds later he was standing in Broad Street in front of the railings, staring up at the big carved faces. The dead stone eyes stared back at him coldly, and the stone beards twinkled with frost.

Joe looked down and saw a tiny black cat sitting on the pavement, its face raised to his expectantly. Its tail was curved like a question mark as if to say, 'I'm ready, Joe. Are you?'

'What do we do first, I wonder?' Joe said aloud, and at once the little cat took a flying leap upwards and landed neatly on the great stone head at the end of the row.

It stayed there for a minute, peeping down through the carved stone curls, dabbing at the long stone nose with its paws, then it leaped onto the next head, and the next, until every one of those seventeen statues had felt the warm, soft paws of the purry little cat on its icy-cold face.

As the cat leapt from head to head something amazing

happened. The faces came to life. One wrinkled its nose and sneezed loudly, another yawned and cleared its throat, a third shook its head violently and opened and shut its mouth several times. Then they all peered round at each other curiously and when they saw their friends were awake too their big stone faces were wreathed in smiles.

But none of them spoke. They were all nodding and winking at each other silently, and looking up at the stars, as if to say, 'It's a fine night, mates!'

Suddenly, Joe remembered the piece of paper. He unfolded it carefully and read it through under a street lamp, then he spoke the simple words aloud, in a firm clear voice:

> *'Stone men of Wales,*
> *Silent so long,*
> *Awake! And thrill this city*
> *With your song!'*

And as the last words of the spell echoed along Broad Street the seventeen men of the Pontybodkin Male Voice Choir opened their mouths, and sang.

Miraculous singing it was, as rich and as mellow as ripe fruit. The great sound rose up and floated out over the frosty rooftops as Joe stood by the railings with the black cat purring in his arms, his whole body tingling as he listened to the most wonderful music he had ever heard.

They warmed up with a few short songs in Welsh, and with *Land of My Fathers* and *Men of Harlech*. Then, after a pause for a bit of coughing and clearing of throats, they burst into a great hymn:

> *'Guide me, O thou great Jehovah,*
> *Pilgrim through this barren land!'*

All along Holywell Street doors were opening, sash windows were being pushed up, heads were popping out. From Catte Street and Ship Street, from George Street and St Giles, people were coming to hear the strange singing, for the miracle of the music had woven itself into their dreams.

In no time at all Broad Street was filled with people in pyjamas, yawning students and landladies in flowery dressing-gowns, all bleary-eyed and happy as they listened, and the Pontybodkin Male Voice Choir sang on and on, making up for all its years of silence with marvellous song, as the clocks of the city crept steadily on towards midnight.

'They'll do *requests*!' the crowds whispered to each other in excitement. 'Let's see if they'll sing something for us. Let's ask for the old favourites. Go on, you ask them . . . no, *you* ask them . . .'

And they sang a Latin school-song for two rumple-headed students in yellow pyjamas:

> *'Gaudeamus igitur*
> *Iuvenes dum sumus!'*

they bellowed joyfully. And they sang *'Pack up your troubles in your old kitbag'* for the park keeper who'd once been a soldier. And for Mrs Mutton, the old widow-lady who lived next door to Joe, they sang a quiet verse of *'God be with you till we meet again'*, and when they sang this the tears rolled down their stone cheeks, and splashed on to the pavement.

49

Suddenly, high up on a tower, a church clock rang out. It was a quarter to twelve. The choir finished Mrs Mutton's request and fell silent. A shiver went through the crowd and people muttered 'Don't pack it up yet, lads. Give us another song!' And the cry was taken up on all sides. 'More! More! We want more!'

'Silence, all of you!' a stern Welsh voice shouted from somewhere at the back. 'There is one more song to come. Silence, and you will hear.' And then the Pontybodkin Male Voice Choir broke into the mightiest song of all:

> *'Hallelujah! Hallelujah!*
> *For the Lord God Omnipotent reigneth!'*

The little black cat had jumped out of Joe's arms and was lost in the crowd. He felt cold suddenly, but then a warm hand was slipped into his. It was the professor.

'Thank you, Joe,' he said. 'You did it. I knew you would.'

> *'And He shall reign for ever and ever!*
> *Hallelujah!'*

the choir sang out. Professor Owen Morgan Jones stood there listening, with the little boy at his side. And the glory of it filled the city.

Joe felt terribly sleepy next day as he hurried along Broad Street, at the last minute as usual. His mum didn't know what a late night they'd had, he and the professor. She slept at the back of their flat, and she hadn't heard a thing.

50

When he looked across the road at the heads Joe half-expected them to have disappeared. But they were there all right, all seventeen of them, and he did think they looked just a little less miserable than usual.

* * *

October the 31st is Hallowe'en, the Eve of the holy day of All Hallows (or All Saints). On Hallowe'en the witches kept their own festival. They rode through the dark on their broomsticks to great witch-feasts. We think of witches as old women wearing tattered black cloaks and pointed black hats, but some were young and beautiful, and dressed in green—the colour of magic and enchantment.

> *Heigh-ho for Hallowe'en!*
> *All the witches to be seen,*
> *Some in black, some in green,*
> *Heigh-ho for Hallowe'en!*

Witches could not usually cross over fresh running water, but they could sail out to sea in eggshell boats and brew up terrible storms. That is why children used to be told that if they had a boiled egg for breakfast or supper, they must break the empty shell with their spoon as soon as they had finished eating.

> *You must break the shell to bits, for fear*
> *The witches should make it a boat, my dear,*
> *For over the sea, away from home,*
> *Far by night the witches roam.*

There were many charms against witchcraft and spells. Making the sign of the cross was one; carrying iron and salt; planting a red-berried rowan tree at your door; or wearing sprigs of the holy herbs—vervain, dill, hyssop and trefoil (clover) whose three-in-one leaf is a symbol of the Trinity.

> *Trefoil, vervain,*
> *John's-wort, dill,*
> *Hinder witches*
> *Of their will.*

* * *

La Belle Dame sans Merci

JOHN KEATS

'O what can ail thee, knight at arms,
　Alone and palely loitering?
The sedge has wither'd from the lake,
　And no birds sing.

O what can ail thee, knight at arms,
　So haggard and so woe-begone?
The squirrel's granary is full
　And the harvest's done.

I see a lily on thy brow
　With anguish moist and fever-dew,
And on thy cheek a fading rose
　Fast withereth too.'

'I met a lady in the meads
  Full beautiful, a faery's child.
Her hair was long, her foot was light,
  And her eyes were wild.

I made a garland for her head,
  And bracelets too, and fragrant zone;
She look'd at me as she did love
  And made sweet moan.

I set her on my pacing steed,
  And nothing else saw all day long
For sidelong would she bend and sing
  A faery's song.

She found me roots of relish sweet
  And honey wild and manna dew,
And sure in language strange she said,
  I love thee true.

She took me to her elfin grot,
  And there she wept and sigh'd full sore,
And there I shut her wild wild eyes
  With kisses four.

And there she lullèd me asleep,
  And there I dream'd—Ah, woe betide!
The latest dream I ever dreamt
  On the cold hill side.

I saw pale kings, and princes too,
  Pale warriors, death-pale were they all;
They cried—'La Belle Dame sans Merci
  Hath thee in thrall!'

I saw their starv'd lips in the gloam
  With horrid warning gapèd wide,
And I awoke, and found me here
  On the cold hill side.

And this is why I sojourn here
  Alone and palely loitering,
Though the sedge is wither'd from the lake
  And no birds sing.'

MAGIC
ANCIENT
AND MODERN

As a huge stone is sometimes seen to lie
Couch'd on the bald top of an eminence;
Wonder to all who do the same espy,
By what means it could thither come, and whence;
So that it seems a thing endued with sense,
Like a sea-beast crawled forth, that on a shelf
Of rock or sand reposeth, there to sun itself . . .

from *Resolution and Independence*

WILLIAM WORDSWORTH

The Mother Stone

ANGELA PICKERING

There is an ancient belief that the earth grows stones, just as it grows potatoes or grass. Suffolk farmers used to say that there was no point in picking the stones off the fields for the earth would only grow more. They believed that stones grew and reproduced just as plants and animals do. A man who lived many years ago at Martlesham in Suffolk kept a piece of rock on his window-sill. He called it 'the mother stone' and believed that the pebbles in the garden were its offspring.

'Look, Ann, he's limping.'

'Who? Jo?'

'No, silly. Not Jo. The horse.'

Ann steadied herself on top of the gate which she had been imagining was a real pony. She shaded her eyes to look over the stony meadow where old Jo's magnificent Suffolk Punch was grazing quietly.

'You're right. Poor old thing!'

In the distance the horse moved on a few steps, one hind leg giving a little under its shaggy fetlock.

'I expect it's a stone,' Carol said. 'The ground's full of them. Could you get it out with one of those spike things like I've got on my guide knife?'

'What? Oh I don't know. Something similar I expect.'

Ann was a little ashamed of herself. She had lived in this part of Suffolk all her life, whereas Carol was a town girl. Yet Carol was the first to notice the horse's leg.

She stared at Carol's neat blue jeans, her tidy hair. She must be nice to this cousin, whose mother was ill and whose father had gone off and left her.

'Ann, don't you think we ought to tell him? He might let us have a ride. What are you thinking about?'

Ann said, 'That Jo'll *never* let you ride the horse. Still, we'd better go over.'

She slid off the gate, but Carol was over before her. Soon they were running across the grass.

'Mind the stones,' Ann puffed. 'Or you'll be the next one.'

They caught up with Jo just as he reached the horse, stopping a few feet away to catch their breath.

The old horse, as grey as its master, nuzzled at the sugar Jo held out for it. The old farmer patted its heavy neck.

He hadn't seemed to notice the girls. Carol gave Ann a nudge.

'Good morning, Jo.'

There was no answer.

'Go on,' hissed Carol.

'Jo,' Ann tried again, summoning up her courage. She never knew where she was with Jo. 'Did you know the horse was lame?'

'Lame?'

Jo turned round, fixing them slowly with his watery eyes.

'Well, at least, we think so. That is, my cousin saw him limping. Of course she might be wrong . . .'

The old man stared at her for a minute, then turned back to the horse. The great animal waited patiently.

'Which one?' he said at last.

Carol pointed and the horse lifted its heavy hind leg with a swift toss of its head as if to confirm their diagnosis.

Jo felt in the sagging pocket of his jacket and pulled out a penknife.

'You see.' Carol hopped on one leg. 'You see. He *is* using that spike thing. I never believed it really did get stones out of horses' hooves. Oh, I wish he'd let me do it.'

Jo straightened his back.

'You ever sat on a horse?' he asked Carol. 'Then come back this time tomorrow when his leg has had a rest like. The old boy'll let you ride on his back. Seeing as you've done him such a favour.'

'Can I really? Oh, thanks. Thanks, Jo.'

Ann kicked at the grass. Jo had never offered her a ride in all the years she'd known him.

'And as you're such a fine young lady,' Jo continued, 'you won't mind doing us both another favour.'

'Of course,' said Carol.

'Then take this here wretched stone, take her down to the beach and throw her out to sea as far as you can.'

'What for?'

'You aren't a country gel so you don't know. Why to drown her, see. That there's a breeding stone, a Mother Stone!'

He opened the palm of his hand and held out the pebble he'd prised from the horse's hoof.

'You do that for me, and you can have as many rides as you like, horse permitting. You and your friend too.'

'Cousin,' said Carol. 'We're cousins.'

'Aye.'

58

He bent his head over the horse, lifting each hoof in turn to look for further stones.

'Go on now, before I change my ideas. Just mind you get rid of that there stone. Would have split the horse apart, she would, given time. Aye.'

The girls turned and ran back across the meadow, smothering their giggles until they were safely over the gate.

'Does he always talk like that?' choked Carol. 'Is it old Suffolk or something? Fancy calling a stone, *HER!*'

'Don't mind him. Jo's all right,' Ann said. 'Come on, let's look at it then. It hardly seems big enough to cause all that trouble.'

'There's plenty more stones in the meadow. The horse could pick up another tomorrow.'

Ann frowned.

'Let's hope not. Poor old horse.'

Carol opened her palm.

'Actually it's quite pretty. I think I'd like to keep it.'

They peered at the stone, which was no more than an inch across and a beautiful pale pink flecked with grey.

'You know what,' Carol said. 'I'm going to start collecting stones while I'm here. There's plenty on the beach and this is a lovely one to begin with.'

'He said you were to drown it,' Ann argued. 'You promised.'

Carol laughed.

'Get rid of it. He only meant me to get rid of it. Anyway it's out of his way now.'

When they got back to the house, Carol put the stone on the bedroom window-sill where it sparkled in the sun.

The next morning it looked even more lovely. It seemed larger, more luminous. Carol stroked it gently.

'I'm so glad I kept it.'

'Hmm,' Ann frowned. 'I still think you should have thrown it in the sea like Jo said.'

They went to the field about ten, but Jo was nowhere in sight.

'He didn't actually say we had to wait for him,' Carol persuaded. 'I'm going to ride the horse *now!*'

The old horse was so docile and stood so quietly, Carol had no trouble leading him to the gate so she could mount.

It was a grand morning. Although the horse went little faster than walking pace it was exhilarating sitting high up on his broad back with the sea sparkling in the distance.

Then Ann had a turn. Only when the old animal showed signs of tiring did they leave him to graze quietly among the stones.

As they left, they saw Jo bent double over the rough brown earth in the next field.

'Drowned her well then?' he called.

Carol giggled.

'You bet!'

'Carol, that was a lie!'

Carol shrugged.

'Well, the stupid old man doesn't know any better. What's he doing anyway?'

'Picking up stones,' Ann explained. 'Otherwise he'd never get the plough through that field. Didn't you see those great piles by the hedge? You think you've got rid of them all, and then the plough turns more of them up each spring. It goes on and on. Almost as if they grow.'

'You don't mean to say Jo still uses the horse to plough with?' Carol asked. 'How medieval!'

'No, silly. Jo's got a tractor. But it's still hard work for an old man.'

'Why doesn't he retire?'

Ann sighed. How could she explain to her cousin? Jo was part of the land. How could he give up his fields, his crops, his very existence?

Later that night Carol leant on the window-sill playing with the stone.

'Do you know,' she said, 'I think it's grown.'

'Nonsense!'

'Come and look.'

Ann peered at the stone.

'Go on,' she laughed. 'You've changed it for another one.'

'No, I haven't. Perhaps *you* have.'

'Of course not.'

'Then it's grown.'

Ann frowned. She wasn't going to argue about a silly trick like that. The new stone was not nearly as pretty. And yet somehow it seemed much the same. Without touching it, she examined the stone carefully, noting the shape of each fleck, each lump, the way it shaded from pink to rose and to pink again.

In the night there was a crash like something dropping. Ann woke with a start. She looked towards the window. Something lay on the floor as if it had rolled off the sill. She tiptoed over. It was the stone.

It had rolled off because the sill was not big enough to hold it any more. Ann shuddered. It could have smashed through the window and into the yard.

There was a rustle from Carol's bed and in a moment Carol had joined her by the window.

'Honest, Ann. I swear I never touched it.'

Ann stared at her cousin's pale face.

'I know you haven't. It's like Jo said. This is a breeding stone. A Mother Stone.'

Carol collapsed on the bed, her feet tucked under her as if she were afraid the stone might attack.

Ann was suddenly practical.

'We must get rid of it!'

'When?'

'As soon as it's light.'

They lay huddled under the bedclothes unable to sleep. At last through the gap in the curtains the sun rose, shining weakly on the stone, making it glow.

They went together to fetch the wheelbarrow from the shed, neither of the girls wanting to be left alone in the bedroom.

They gasped at the size of the stone. It was already too heavy to lift. Wrapping their hands in sweaters, for they shrank from touching it with bare hands, they rolled the stone to the stairs. It bounced down, narrowly missing a vase in the hall. With great difficulty they scooped it into the barrow, hurrying in case Ann's parents awoke.

'Where?' asked Carol, licking her lips. But she already knew.

'To the sea. We must drown it.'

There was no one about. They pushed the stone along

the lane. It was swelling visibly now and every step was an effort.

'Quick!' urged Ann. 'There isn't much time.'

'I can't!' wailed Carol, as they paused for breath before Jo's meadow. 'I can't!'

She collapsed panting on the handle of the barrow.

'We must!'

Suddenly the barrow tipped with Carol's extra weight, and the stone flew out. The frayed rope holding the gate gave way and the stone rolled through, gathering speed across the dewy grass.

The old horse watched it with frightened eyes, stepping out of its way like a young colt, then kicking up his shaggy heels to canter wildly round and round.

In the middle of the meadow the stone stopped, jerked once and began to split. Fragments flew in all directions, till nothing of it was left. Yet it seemed that the meadow was even stonier than usual. Hundreds of small grey pebbles, baby stones, its offspring, lay in the long grass.

A few weeks later Ann wrote to her cousin:

'Dear Carol, I'm glad you like your new school and Auntie Jill is so much better. I'm sorry you won't be coming to stay just yet, but if you did, you'd find a lot of things have changed.

'Old Jo has retired after all and they took the horse away. I tried to persuade Dad to have him but it was no good. After you left, Jo took to dumping his stones on the beach every day. A tractor-load at a time. It took ages. Poor old man! There were so many of them . . .'

Ann paused, sucking her pen. She was about to write,

'*In the end the stones got too much for him, you see. I hope you're satisfied!*'

But at the last moment she changed her mind. She ought to feel sorry for Carol, what with her mother being ill and her father going away.

Instead she felt rather sorrier for the horse!

Tilly Witch in the Park

PAT KREMER

Tilly Witch sat on a bench in the park eating a pink whippy ice-cream. Scuffle, her black cat, sat alongside, licking drips with a small, quick tongue. The sun shone brightly. Families lay quietly on the grass on rugs; children played, parents snoozed, young boys and girls chatted; it was very peaceful.

Tilly Witch sighed—she was bored. Witch business was not very good these days. Few people came to consult her in her neat little council flat. Very occasionally she was called upon to find lost dogs or rings. Sometimes she cured bad tummies or headaches. But these were dull spells—there had been very little chance to try out some interesting ones recently. Ingredients, too, were difficult to find. She knew where to search for spiders' webs and mouse whiskers—she crept round people's greenhouses and cellars, probing into the darkest and dustiest corners; and she searched church belfries to retrieve bats' wings (from ones that had already died, of course). But she had stopped collecting frog-spawn since reading that it had become very scarce, and she felt it was cruel to dig for wriggly, fat worms. Life was very difficult—modern times were no good for real old-fashioned witches.

Glumly, she reached for her Spell Book, which she always carried in her plastic bag.

'Newts . . . breasts of robins . . . legs of toads . . . wings of butterflies . . . tongues of mice . . . .'

Tilly Witch shuddered. She read on. Her finger rested at Chapter 215. She smiled—this looked better: 'How to Restore Lost Youth.' Next to it was another good one: 'How to Create a Sea-Monster.'

Interesting and, looking at the ingredients, possible.

Perhaps—here and now—why not?

She crouched behind some shrubs and whispered to the cat.

Scuffle ran around collecting rose petals and crab apples, empty snail-shells and a soft bird's feather, gleaming red berries and emerald pond slime, frothy spider's spit and sharp holly prickles. Tilly Witch flung them into an empty plant pot and began to stir them with a stick. She added three drops of rain water from a puddle and ten drops of dew from a shiny, cupped leaf growing in the darkest, coolest corner of the park.

'Six centipede's legs, six centipede's legs,' she muttered. But when Scuffle dropped the wriggly, tickly insect into her hand she looked at it for a while and then replaced it under a damp log.

'We'll just have to try to make it work without,' she said, and began softly to sing the spells; the Earth Spirits' Spell first, and then the Water Spirits'.

The softest of grey mists rose from the plant pot.

A small boy was watching her curiously, fishing-net in hand: 'You're a witch, aren't you?'

But before Tilly Witch had time to reply, his big sister pulled him away: 'Don't be rude, Tom. There aren't any witches nowadays.'

Scuffle dipped her tail into the plant pot and swished it around, three times. Then she ran up the tallest tree whose great branches stretched wide across the park and she flashed in and out among the leaves. Round and round whirled her tail and a cascade of rainbow-tinted droplets spun through the air onto the grass.

Mr Bannerjee, who had left his dress shop for the afternoon to bring his mother, wife and baby to the park, put out his hand, palm upward, and glanced at the blue sky twinkling through the leaves.

'That's strange. It feels like rain,' he said.

He had been very busy in the shop selling clothes and putting away new stock. He had been feeling quite old and tired.

Some children ran up with a ball—Joshua, Helen and Derek. Mr Bannerjee flicked out his foot very quickly, the ball rose high in the air and seemed to loop the loop before it fell back again in front of him.

'Cor, Mister, that's great!' said Joshua, wide-eyed.

Mr Bannerjee was as amazed himself. He felt more excited and energetic than he could ever remember. He stood up. So, all around him, did Grandmas and Mums and other Dads. He kicked the ball again and it curved and swerved along the grass. A Grandma jumped at it and sent it spinning between two flower-beds.

'Goal!' she shouted.

Never had there been such a match! Goal-posts were made from walking-sticks. Old men and ladies straightened out creaking joints and took up their positions on the field. Little children dashed in between. There was shouting and calling and movement everywhere. The ball seemed alive as it twisted and rolled from foot to foot. The ice-cream man and the park keeper stood amazed.

Meanwhile, the rainbow rain kept falling, pitting the surface of the pond with tiny circles of reflecting light. The children, poking with sticks by the edge, in between the empty sandwich bags and crumpled cans, stopped in amazement. Shafts of sunlight caught the scales of tiny golden fish. The brown minnows and sticklebacks had been transformed.

'Eee, someone's emptied a goldfish bowl in 'ere!' gasped a child.

Tom scooped up his fishing-net and tipped the contents into his jam jar.

'It's a monster!' he gasped. The tiny creature had three golden humps and a forked tail. It stared solemnly at Tom through the glass and he fed it with crumbs of vinegar crisps and wafer biscuits.

Tilly Witch rubbed her bony fingers together with satisfaction.

Shadows lengthened. Everyone, with flushed, happy faces, sat on the grass together. Ice-cream and sandwiches were shared around, names and addresses were exchanged.

There was laughter and chatter, and hands were

shaken, and backs were slapped, as people, regretfully, made their way out of the park to go home for their suppers.

It was quiet again.

Tilly Witch smiled as she tucked her Spell Book in her shopping-bag. The magic was beginning to wear off now. She hadn't used the centipede's legs, of course, and they were good for strengthening spells; but even without them it had been a very good day.

Tom, on his way home, peered hard into his glass jar. The monster had disappeared—there were only a few surprised minnows swimming round a soggy crisp packet. He frowned, shrugged his shoulders and ran after his sister.

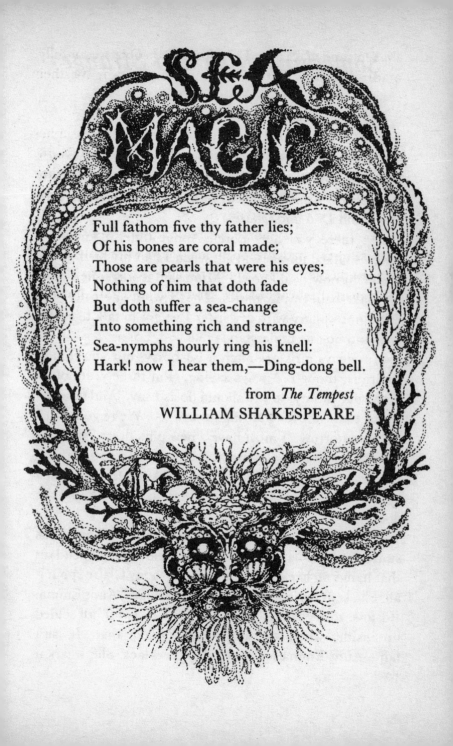

SEA MAGIC

Full fathom five thy father lies;
Of his bones are coral made;
Those are pearls that were his eyes;
Nothing of him that doth fade
But doth suffer a sea-change
Into something rich and strange.
Sea-nymphs hourly ring his knell:
Hark! now I hear them,—Ding-dong bell.

from *The Tempest*
WILLIAM SHAKESPEARE

Something Rich and Strange

IRENE HOLNESS

Lorel? Are you there? It's Jimmy! Come on, the water's lovely and warm here at the edge of the sea, now the tide is out. Hurry! Aunt Emma will be down in a minute with Mum and Dad and Claire.

Oh, there you are, Lorel! About time! I know we haven't talked for ages. Well, when I had my birthday— I'm eight now, you know!—Mum said it was time I gave up make-believe playmates. That's what she calls you. But I'm so angry with my sister I've got to talk to someone, and no one understands like you, Lorel.

Mum says girls are often a bit bossy, but you're not. Claire is, though. Always saying, 'I'm three years older than you, Jimmy, so you should do as I say.' And now she seems to be forever wanting things, too. We're going to a party tomorrow. 'I must have a new pink dress,' she kept on. She'd already got a dress. A blue one. I know why the new one had to be pink. To match Aunt Emma's shell necklace, because Claire wants that, as well. I know she does.

It's lovely living near Aunt Emma. She tells marvellous stories and lets us listen to the sea in the big shell pendant that hangs on her shell necklace. But today Claire spoilt it all. She kept saying, 'I do like your necklace, Aunt Emma. I'd love to try it on.' It makes me feel awful, all folded up inside, when she keeps hinting like that. It isn't fair—Aunt Emma loves her shell necklace. She wears it all the time because it belonged to her mother—our great-grandmother, because Aunt Emma is really Dad's aunt, you see. And the necklace is part of her best story. Not the one about the chosen baby adopted by a kind mother and father. That's Claire's favourite. Mine's the one about Great-Grandmother and the magic—oh, I've told you so many times before! All right then, just like Aunt Emma tells it. . . .

Our Great-Grandmother's name was Margaret. When she was young, Margaret found a beautiful trumpet on the beach near here. It was really a curly sea-shell with a stone-with-a-hole-in-the-middle for the mouthpiece. When Margaret blew on the trumpet, the sound it made was strange and sweet. And someone answered, singing the same tune. It was a mermaid. At least, Margaret was sure she was a mermaid, though the sea was choppy and foamy, and she had only one quick glimpse of a shining tail.

'Give me back my trumpet,' the mermaid called, and so Margaret tossed it to her, though she really would have liked to keep it. Then the mermaid sat on a rock, with white spray all around her like a lacy skirt. She pulled a long golden hair from her head and threaded a necklace of pink sea-shells, with one big shell dangling from the middle.

She threw the necklace to Margaret and sang:

> *'These shells fine pearls forever shall be,*
> *Owned by you or other lady*
> *Of your blood and family.'*

Margaret put on the necklace, and the mermaid waved and disappeared under the sea.

So Margaret went home. When she looked in the mirror, the shells had turned into pearls. Margaret wore the pearls at her wedding to our great-grandfather. They had a baby boy who was going to be our Grandad, and then they thought it would be nice to have a little girl, too, so along came Aunt Emma.

When Great-Grandmother Margaret died, she left the pearls to Aunt Emma, only the magic had worn off by then and they were shells again. Aunt Emma always laughs when she gets to this bit, Lorel. I don't believe she thinks it's—

Oh, they're calling! I must go. See you tomorrow, after the party. I'll tell you if Claire gets the necklace.

Hallo again, Lorel. Mum said I wasn't to come in the sea today, because it's chilly. While I was running down to the beach to meet you I thought I heard music. I expect it was the wind. Don't you love the way the wind picks up the tops of the waves and pulls them into the air, all fluffy and white, like sea-snow? Hey, Lorel! Don't splash. Mum will think I've been paddling. Sorry, I was teasing. You want to know about the necklace.

Well, Claire got all dressed up in her pink frock, with her hair done and everything, and she didn't look too bad, really. No, she isn't prettier than you. She's got sort of browny-red hair, and I like yellow hair like yours best.

Anyway, Mum said to show ourselves to Aunt Emma on the way to the party. 'You both look very smart,' Aunt Emma said and—Lorel—she took off the shell necklace and put it round Claire's neck.

'I've worn it for a long time,' she said, 'Now it's yours, Claire.'

Sisters are very peculiar. Claire said 'Thank you' ever so quietly. She held the shell pendant—the one you can hear the sea in—and whispered, 'I shall always think of this one as your shell, Aunt Emma.'

Then she brightened up and ran over to the big mirror in the corner, and—well, something a bit scary happened next. I could see Claire and Aunt Emma in the mirror. It's darkish in the corner, but their faces looked white and their eyes were big and round, as if they were very surprised or frightened. Then I saw the necklace. It was all shining and shimmery. The shells had changed to pearls. Don't laugh, Lorel. They had! Except for the special shell pendant, the one Claire said would always be Aunt Emma's.

Then Aunt Emma did an odd thing. She stood behind Claire, touched the necklace and said the mermaid's rhyme:

> *'These shells fine pearls forever shall be,*
> *Owned by you or other lady*
> *Of your blood and family.*

You remember my story about the chosen baby, Claire?'

'The baby was you, Aunt Emma?' That's what Claire answered, as though she already knew.

Aunt Emma nodded. She said, 'I was always so proud of being chosen. So you see, though I was adopted into your great-grandmother's family, I was not of her blood. But you are.'

My sister took off that wonderful shining thing and spoke very clearly.

'This is still yours, Aunt Emma. Please keep it until I'm grown up.'

Aunt Emma looked ever so happy—not just about having the necklace back, but pleased with Claire, too, like I was.

She bent down and Claire put the necklace on for her, and I saw that it was just a string of pink shells, after all.

Before we went to the party, Aunt Emma let me listen to the special shell. But instead of the sea, it was beautiful faraway music I heard.

I can hear it again now—only louder! Hey, Lorel! Where did you get that trumpet? From your great-grandmother? Oh, Lorel, don't dive home beneath the waves yet! 'Bye then. See you tomorrow.

Overheard on a Saltmarsh

HAROLD MONRO

Nymph, nymph, what are your beads?
Green glass, goblin. Why do you stare at them?
Give them me.
                No.
Give them me. Give them me.
                        No.
Then I will howl all night in the reeds,
Lie in the mud and howl for them.

Goblin, why do you love them so?

They are better than stars or water,
Better than voices of winds that sing,
Better than any man's fair daughter,
Your green glass beads on a silver ring.

Hush, I stole them out of the moon.

Give me your beads, I desire them.
                              No.

I will howl in a deep lagoon
For your green glass beads, I love them so.
Give them me. Give them.
                              No.

The Sea-Morgan's Baby

RUTH L. TONGUE

*This is a story from Somerset told to Ruth Tongue in 1916 by
a woman who had heard it from her granny. A morgan is a
water-spirit.*

There was a fisherman come down in the owl-light into
St Audries Bay. He'd heard someone singing down there
in the dark and he were curious. So he come down by all

75

a-tiptoe. But he couldn't be quiet enough if he tried and the sea-morgans was all away off the rocks and into the tide, but in their hurry they left a baby morgan a-kicking and chuckling under the cliff waterfall and the fisherman found her.

His heart was sore for a little daughter he'd just left in Watchet churchyard and his wife's heart were a-broke. So he takes the baby morgan whoame up over to the farm and puts her in the empty cradle, and his wife took to her at once though she couldn't ever get the little creature's hair dry—not properly dry even in sun and hill wind, and it smelled of the sea.

The baby grew up like they all do, and, except that she would be forever paddling and dabbling in the spring-pond and the trout-stream, she made 'en a real good daughter till a neighbour came pushing her nose in.

'Dear, dear, how wet your hair be. Go and dry it like a Christian.' But the girl just laughed. Then the neighbour had to go and say, 'A girt girl like you a-paddling in the spring-pond an't Christian at all. You go down to the sea and have a swim there.'

The old couple bustled the meddler out and as she went she heard a queer song, coming from the far-away sea. 'What ever be that?' she asked, but they wouldn't say and she heard it again behind her and it was the girl singing. 'That's my song,' she say. 'Someone wants me. There will be a storm tonight.'

Well, that meddler ran and roused the Doniford and Staple men to chase away this witch—but the girl ran away from them all, laughing. They couldn't catch up with her, and then they heard the song and the waves was thundering on the rocks and they bided where they was up on the cart-track. They heard her singing as she ran out along the rocks and then a great wave took her and no one ever saw her again.

The Moon-Child

FIONA MACLEOD

A little lonely child am I
    That have not any soul:
God made me as the homeless wave,
    That has no goal.

A seal my father was, a seal
    That once was man;
My mother loved him tho' he was
    'Neath mortal ban.

He took a wave and drownèd her,
    She took a wave and lifted him:
And I was born where shadows are
    In sea-depths dim.

All through the sunny blue-sweet hours
    I swim and glide in waters green:
Never by day the mournful shores
    By me are seen.

But when the gloom is on the wave
   A shell unto the shore I bring:
And then upon the rocks I sit
   And plaintive sing.

I have no playmate but the tide
   The seaweed loves with dark brown eyes:
The night-waves have the stars for play,
   For me but sighs.

He put his acorn helmet on;
It was plumed of the silk of the thistledown;
The corselet plate that guarded his breast
Was once the wild bee's golden vest;
His cloak, of a thousand mingled dyes,
Was formed of the wings of butterflies;
And the quivering lance which he brandished bright,
Was the sting of a wasp he had slain in fight.

Swift he bestrode his firefly steed;
He bared his blade of the bent-grass blue;
He drove his spurs of the cockle-seed,
And away like a glance of thought he flew,
To skim the heavens, and follow far
The fiery trail of the rocket star.

from *An Elfin Knight*

JOSEPH RODMAN DRAKE

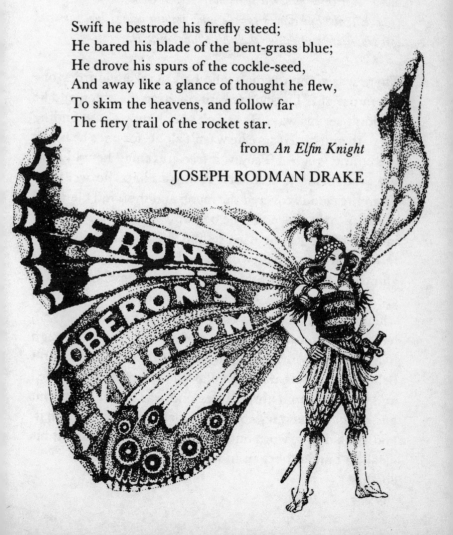

FROM OBERON'S KINGDOM

The Travelling Tree

RUTH L. TONGUE

This folk tale from Kent was written down fifty years ago, but the story is much older than that. It goes back to the seventeenth century, and is over three hundred years old. 'Robin Goodfellow' or 'Puck' (two Elizabethan names for the same impish being) loved to trick lost travellers and could 'shift his shape' at will.

There was a countryman who had to take a journey one autumn night. The clouds kept covering the moon and he couldn't see his way. He wasn't very happy about finding his path and he felt sure he wasn't alone, for once he heard something laugh. ''Tis just a tree creaking,' he told himself, and being a stubborn Kentish chap, he went on. Then the clouds covered the moon and the wind blew and the rain came down and he couldn't see a hands-breadth in front of him, so he tried to find shelter for a bit.

There wasn't a hedge on those hills, but he thought he glimpsed a tree, threshing its branches in the gale. He groped for it but the clouds kept covering the moon and when he climbed up it wasn't there, but further on. Well, he walked after it nigh a mile and again he heard a laugh like a creaking branch, but being stubborn he wouldn't believe his own ears and followed on again. He walked and walked about three miles and was blown all about and drenched and icy cold, but at last he got a hand on it, and sunk down, worn out, in its shelter, and huddled his cloak to him and began to warm up.

Then he heard a voice: 'I dunno what you plan to do,' said the tree, 'but I'm getting wet to the bone. I'm going home to a nice fire.'

And it went.

Robin Goodfellow

From Oberon in Fairyland,
The King of ghosts and shadows there,
Mad Robin I, at his command,
Am sent to view the night-sports here:
      What revel rout
      Is kept about
In every corner where I go—
      I will o'er sea
      And merry be,
And make good sport with ho, ho, ho!

More swift than lightning can I fly
About this airy welkin soon,
And in a minute's space descry
Each thing that's done below the moon.
      There's not a hag
      Or ghost shall wag
Or cry 'Ware goblins' where I go;
      But Robin I
      Their feats will spy
And send them home with ho, ho, ho!

Whene'er such wanderers I meet
As from their night-sports they trudge home,
With counterfeiting voice I greet
And call them on with me to roam
　　Through woods, through lakes,
　　Through bogs, through brakes;
　Or else unseen with them I go,
　　All in the nick
　　To play some trick
And frolic it with ho, ho, ho!

Sometimes I meet them like a man,
Sometimes an ox, sometimes a hound,
And to a horse I turn me can
To trip and trot about them round—
　　But if to ride
　　My back they stride,
More swift than wind away I go,
　　O'er hedge and lands,
　　Through pools and ponds,
I whirry, laughing, ho, ho, ho!

The Grig's Red Cap

RUTH L. TONGUE

A folk tale from Middlesex, which Ruth Tongue heard from an old groom at Stanmore, called Harry White, in 1936. A 'harnet' is a hornet.

There were two labourers crossing Stanmore Common when the grigs were playing in the bracken. Two of the grigs put on their red caps and vanished but the third was in such a panic that he pulled the red cap too hard and he fell into it like a sack. Then all he could do was keep still till the men passed on, but one of them saw the red hat.

'Here's luck,' said he. 'A nice, large, red cap.'

'Leave it lay,' says t'other man.

'Not me—I'm needing a smart hat myself.'

'Leave it lay,' says his mate, very worried.

But no, not he. He puts it on right over his ears and if the grig was unhappy before, now he couldn't even breathe. He began to kick and twist and pull hair and thump, and so did the labourer only he gave himself the beating.

His mate watched him while he yelled, 'There's the father and mother of all harnets inside it, and don't I know it.'

And somehow he dragged it off.

The red cap was out of his reach in a second and something shot out of it and was gone with it crying, 'You was told to leave it lay.'

Then all the bracken rang with grig laughter and the men ran like hell.

THREE WISHES

Moon light
Moon bright
New moon
Seen tonight
I wish I may
I wish I might
Have the wish
I wish tonight

Something in the Wind

MARGARET JOY

Emmy's knees were bunched up against her chest, and her legs were sticking over the green velvet arms of the comfortable old chair. 'Emmy!' called her mother's voice faintly from two flights of stairs below. 'Emmy, get ready for bed now!'

Emmy mumbled something obediently, but kept her eyes on the words as she turned over another page. She was so tightly curled up that she couldn't shout an answer anyway.

Besides, she'd had a rotten day at school and needed to escape from it for a while. First of all, her best ink cartridge had run out right in the middle of the Maths test, so Miss Goodbody had taken off marks because it was finished in pencil. Then in Cookery she'd really been making an effort to do everything step by step as Mrs Hardy liked it, so she found she was the last to finish and had to spend all of Break washing up and wiping the stoves down. Then that stupid Charlie Robson had been chalking on the back of her blazer coming down the stairs, so she'd hurried and fallen off the last step and twisted her ankle. So *then* she had had to miss her favourite Netball lesson.

'It's not fair,' murmured Emmy to herself, pushing her long dark hair back from her face and closing her book. 'Things always go wrong, and school's so boring just at the moment—always the same thing day after day.

Everything's so . . . so predictable. I wish something *interesting* would happen . . .'

Her joints clicked as she stiffly unrolled herself from the chair and stood up. She should have switched the light on ages ago: it was quite dark. She pushed open the casement window and looked out. The wind was whistling round the side of the house. Down in the field beyond the garden, bushes and hedges were swaying in the wind, first this way, then that, tossing their branches in a wild hula-hula dance.

Suddenly across the dim field raced two small shadowy creatures. They bounded across the grass, leaping over tussocks in a mad chase. Emmy stared: hares, she thought. They were leaping over thistles, chasing one another, running round in frenzied circles before galloping off at amazing speed.

'Mad March hares,' thought Emmy. '*They*'re not bored!'

She had a wild urge to run down the stairs and race round the field with them, letting the wind blow her this way and that. . . .

Cloud shadows crossed the field and she looked up at the sky. A narrow, shining moon gleamed like a silver nail paring on black velvet. 'The new moon!' realised Emmy. Her heart seemed to give an extra, excited beat: 'I can wish!' She looked up again at the thin silver moon. It was hidden behind fast-blown shreds of cloud, appeared again for an instant—

'Em-my!' called her mother. Quick! She must wish! But what for? She didn't really know—just something. She looked down at the shadowy March hares still tumbling and racing along with the wind. 'Oh, I don't know,' she said aloud to the new moon. 'I just *wish* . . . !'

On the way to school Emmy felt different. Something was going to happen; she knew something was in the wind. She held her raincoat round her, feeling oddly excited.

The first lesson was Biology. They were studying the way birds fly. Emmy was surprised to learn that birds' wings were formed very much like human arms, ending in five fingers.

Next, Geography. Mr Riddick had brought some slides to show them. 'There are several kinds of cloud formation,' he pointed out. 'These are the rolling, fat, cushiony ones. They're called cumulus clouds and they often mean that rain is on the way.'

Emmy was quite surprised when the bell went for Break.

She fetched her raincoat and ran outside; she was beginning to have that strange excited feeling again.

The school was built on rising ground. Green fields sloped gently down to the outskirts of the town. The flat expanse of grey playground suddenly reminded Emmy of a runway. The one-storey school was the air terminal: the flat roof was the spectators' terrace and the Head's room up above there, was the control tower.

Emmy burst out laughing and raced across the playground. She hadn't done her raincoat up and it flapped and cracked behind her as the wind caught it. Her hair streamed back and she leaned forward into the wind, feeling it push against her. She was still racing, racing, faster, faster, her feet barely touching the ground, nearly at the end of the playground, the noise of the wind roaring in her ears, then . . .

Her racing feet had left the ground, her raincoat was billowing in the strong wind: she was air-borne!

She had never felt anything like this before. She was resting on air, able to see the world spread out below her. It was marvellous, incredible! She wanted to fly on and on, for ever and ever, free as air . . .

'Wait for me-e!' A faint shout came from somewhere behind. She managed to turn her head slightly and then couldn't believe her eyes: it was that awful Charlie Robson! His scarlet-lined parka was flapping furiously round him as he tried to catch up with her.

'Wait for u-u-us!' came more faint cries. The wind tugged at Emmy's hair as she turned again. A flock of flapping figures was taking off from the playground, swirling and whirling up towards her: it was Kathy and Joanne and Robert and—'It's all my class!' gasped Emmy.

The wind roared and tossed them higher and higher. Their ears vibrated with the noise. An extra-strong gust blew Joanne closer to Emmy. 'What's happening?' shouted Joanne.

'It was the new moon—I wished!' shouted Emmy through gulps of air.

'Look out!' shouted Charlie Robson, flapping just be-hind them. He was looking fearfully over his shoulder. A huge, billowing, cushiony cloud was catching up with them, tattered and torn at the edges by the teeth of the wind.

Suddenly it was all round them, enveloping them in a

grey damp mist. Kathy disappeared from sight; Joanne was swallowed up by the whiteness. The roar of the wind was muffled by the blanketing cloud. Emmy shuddered as the clammy mist imprisoned her in a silent world.

And then it began to rain.

The cloudy vapours round her began to form into droplets which trickled down her long hair, down her raincoat, into her shoes. She was soaking. And then she realised that the cloud was no longer supporting her. The rain was pouring down from above, falling from the clouds, and she was falling with it, dropping swiftly down through the clouds, sinking, sinking . . .

'You're *covered* in sweat!' said her mother's voice. She was dabbing at Emmy's face with a damp flannel. 'You've probably caught your death of cold, going to bed with that casement wide open—and on such a wild and windy night too!'

Emmy blinked up at her mother from far away. 'It rained,' she whispered. 'We were having a lovely time and then it rained.'

'Yes,' beamed her mother, not listening: 'And you know why it rained, don't you? The garden was getting like a dust-bowl with all the wind we've had lately, and it was driving the hares wild—it was time everything had a real good soak.'

She laughed. 'So I wished.'

'You wished?' said Emmy faintly.

'Yes, there was a new moon last night—didn't you notice it?—so I wished for rain. And now it's pouring down!'

She laid Emmy's clean school blouse ready on the bed. 'Just shows that old superstitious magic really works sometimes, doesn't it?'

Fairy Godmother?

PAMELA SYKES

On the first day of August, Mary was cross.

The next day she was more cross, and felt hot and a sort of all-overish-not-well.

The third day she was very cross indeed and very hot and even less well.

Her mother made her stay in bed and the doctor came. He took her temperature, found lots of tiny little spots on her chest, and said, 'Measles, I'm afraid. You must stay in bed, drink lots of cold drinks, and not see any of your friends till you are quite well again.'

He and her mother left the bedroom together, and when the door had closed behind them, Mary stuck her tongue out at it.

She began to feel more and more ill as more and more little spots appeared.

She was lonely because she could hear her friends laughing in the playground across the road without her.

Her head ached, her arms ached, her legs ached and her eyes ached.

Worst of all, she hated the heat. There were lovely blue

skies and a bright sun outside, but Mary was so hot that she felt as if she were melting like a candle.

Her mother was very kind. She drew the curtains to keep the bedroom cooler. She brought up the radio for Mary to listen to. She offered to read aloud to Mary, her favourite stories. She made big jugs of lemonade from real lemons, which is much nicer than the kind you can buy in shops. She often straightened the bedclothes, and turned the pillow over to try to make Mary cooler.

I wish I could say that Mary was grateful for all this, and nice to her mother, but she wasn't.

In fact, she was really nasty. She said the drawn curtains made the room like a cave, that listening to the radio made her head ache worse, and she was tired of her favourite books. She refused to drink the lemonade—though she would have rather liked to. She said it was too sour. After her mother had stirred some sugar into it, Mary said it was too sweet. When her mother tidied the bedclothes, Mary said she *liked* them tangled. She was very rude and very sorry for herself.

The doctor came each day, but every time he took the thermometer from her mouth he shook his head. 'You're not ready to get up yet,' he told her. 'But if you're a good girl and do what you're told you'll soon be getting better.'

Mary sighed. 'I *wish* I could feel cool again,' she said.

After the doctor had gone her mother came back and *she* sighed as well.

'I know.' She suddenly looked brighter. 'We'll see if your Fairy Godmother can help!'

Now, of course, Mary did not have a real Fairy God-mother. Only people in stories, like Cinderella, are as lucky as that. But Mary's Godmother was so clever at cheering people up, and thinking of lovely surprises and treats, that she did seem almost magic, so she was nick-named 'Fairy Godmother' in the family.

'I'll bet even *she* can't help this time,' said Mary, and turned on her side and sulked.

All the same her mother rang up Mary's 'Fairy God-mother' and told her all about the trouble. Godmother said she would send round a present for Mary at once, which she did.

'She said it was very very special,' her mother told Mary. 'You must keep it carefully and look at it often.' She handed her a flat square package.

Eagerly, Mary ripped off the wrapping. What exciting thing could it possibly be?

It was only a picture. A very pretty one of a wood in springtime, but Mary was disappointed. No picture could cure her horrible hot crossness.

Even her mother seemed a little puzzled, but she said: 'This seems rather odd, but let's hang it up where you can easily see it from your bed, and don't forget to look at it.'

Mary did look at the picture, and by evening she began to realise what a cool picture it was. The trees leaned across a dark but inviting path.

'Oh' thought Mary, 'how lovely to be in such a lovely place, instead of this hot bed.'

She found herself looking at the picture more and more during the evening, and then, after her mother had settled her for the night, a chink of a bright sunset still showed through the drawn curtains.

As she looked . . . and looked . . . Mary began to wonder

where this lovely place was, and wished she could be there.

And as she drifted into sleepiness she found herself imagining that she could feel the refreshing breeze. . . . She was walking along the cool, winding path under the trees. It was lovely not to feel hot after such a long time. Mary began to take notice of the flowers at her feet.

There were white wood-anemones, the colour of snow, clusters of snowdrops, bluebells making a carpet under which sprouted brave little clusters of white and mauve violets. There were catkins above her and primroses opening amongst the dewy undergrowth.

Mary was enchanted. After the fearful heat she had suffered for days, it was glorious to feel the cool scented breeze, and hear it rustling the newly-budding branches. She wandered vaguely for some time growing more and more happy, but also tempted. She knew that the little flowers at her feet would be happiest where they grew naturally, but she longed to pick some. At last, though feeling a little guilty, she did so.

'I must put them in water at once,' was her last thought.

Then suddenly she was wide awake in her own bedroom and her mother was popping the thermometer into her mouth. When she removed it, she looked delighted.

'Much lower, nearly normal!' she exclaimed happily. 'Mary, you're getting well again!'

'I know,' said Mary. 'I don't feel hot any more. In fact, I'm hungry! Do you know,' she went on before her mother could speak, 'it was because of that picture! Godmother must be really magic after all! I remember walking into that springtime wood . . . it was beautifully windy and it made me feel so much better . . .'

'A dream,' said her mother, soothingly. 'But if you feel hungry you can have some breakfast now. Would you like a boiled egg, or——'

Suddenly she stopped speaking.

She looked at the glass of water on the table beside Mary's bed. In it clustered a little bunch of wood violets, primroses, and catkins, all freshly covered with dew.

'Mary!' exclaimed her mother in astonishment. 'Where did these come from? At *this* time of year!'

Christmas Crackers
MARJORIE DARKE

I like Christmas. Usually it's great, but this year nothing went right. Mum had flu, we forgot to put the Christmas pud on in time, Lucy made lumpy custard and Budge emptied the lot over his high chair. The turkey was okay though. Me and Dad cooked that. All the same, Christmas dinner didn't taste right with Mum in bed. After, we kept arguing about which telly programmes to watch—in whispers because Mum's head was splitting. By tea-time everyone felt Christmas was a wash-out.

'Biscuits in the blue tin, Luce,' Dad said brightly. 'Box of crackers in the sideboard, Steve,' and to Budge: 'Come and help me get the cake.'

We knew he was trying to cheer us up, but joining in

was difficult. Budge didn't try. He just sucked his thumb. But, then, he's only a baby.

We had tea on the floor. None of us could be bothered to set the table. Just as well because Lucy fell over pulling her cracker, which made everyone laugh and feel a bit better. Inside the crackers were paper hats and presents and riddles.

Lucy pushed her crown out of her eyes to read: *'What can go up a chimney down, but not down a chimney up?'*

I'd seen that in a comic. 'Umbrella.'

She snorted like she does when anyone gets the better of her. 'Go on, then, Bighead, read yours.'

'It's a daft poem,' I said. *'Wind whistle—Gale blow—Spell my name—Then I'll know.* Know what?'

'The answer, silly.'

'All right, Clever, what's the answer then?'

'I didn't say I *knew*, I only said what the riddle *meant*.'

'Same thing,' I pointed out.

'The answers are on the back,' Dad said in a shut-up-Steve voice.

I looked. 'Just my Christmas luck. They've forgotten to print it! What am I supposed to do . . . spell S.P.E.L.L.?'

'Stop moaning.' Lucy held out a little plastic black cat charm. 'Your whistle's better than this. At least it makes a noise. Blow!'

I blew, but the only sound was the phone ringing. Dad had Budge on his knee, playing a game with him and his little cracker dinosaur toy, so I got up to answer.

'Is that you, Stephen?' asked a man's voice.

'Yes.'

'Good, good. Phoning to let you know I'm catching the

one-fifteen flight. Touch-down at two.'

My brain felt full of Christmas stodge. 'Touch-down?'

The voice said: 'Yes, touch-down. You know . . .
Arrival!' in a brisk sort of way, as if I was being thick.

'Who's speaking?' I asked.

'Ernest, of course. See you near two. I'd like to be more
precise, but when Martha pilots there's no knowing!
Oh . . . give my love to Lucy.' There was a click and the
line went dead before I could ask did he mean Boxing Day
afternoon and what airport and who was Martha?

'Wrong number,' Dad said after I'd told him. 'We
don't know any Ernests or Marthas,' and he began reading us a Brer Rabbit story, doing crazy voices till we fell
about laughing.

After that it was bed-time.

I woke in the dark with Lucy shaking my shoulder. 'Steve
. . . wake up, can't you! Steve!'

I tried to get back into this great dream I was having
about a cream doughnut, and buried my head under the
pillow.

She dragged the pillow away. 'Steve, there's a man on
the balcony.'

'Burglartelldad . . .'

'STEVE!' Yanking off the bedclothes she gave me such
a shove I nearly fell on to the floor.

I shouted: 'Lemmealone!'

But she just grabbed my pyjama jacket and began
tugging me towards the hall. 'He's got a bowler hat, and
an umbrella that he keeps knocking on the window with,
and he's pulling faces at Budge'n me.'

Lucy and Budge share the bedroom that looks out on to the balcony.

'Burglars don't knock,' I said. And only then did it hit me that there's no way on to that balcony except *through* their bedroom—our flat being eight floors up in the tower block, and the fire-escape on the kitchen side.

Lucy had left the door open and as we got to it our eyes nearly fell out with surprise. Running round Budge's cot rail like a live mouse was the dinosaur he'd got out of his cracker. *Nobody making it work!* Budge, standing up clutching the rail, was giggling like mad every time the thing scampered over his fingers. Watching from the other side of the cot was this tall thin man in a pin-striped suit and bowler, holding an umbrella.

He smiled at us. 'Hallo! Budge said to come in. Hope you don't mind . . . as you two sent the messages,' he added, and hooked his umbrella handle over a moonbeam shining between the curtains. With a flick of his wrist he sent the silver light sliding on to the umbrella spike and wrote:

'*STEVE LUCY BUDGE HAPPY CHRISTMAS*'
in the air, just as if it was a Biro. The letters hung glittering like sparklers.

I hadn't a clue what he was talking about and Lucy looked blank. I mean—Budge can't talk that much. And what messages? Who was this weirdie anyway?

As if he'd tuned into my brain, he clicked his tongue, tapping a finger on my forehead. Somehow, when he took his hand away, he was holding a pad with DON'T FORGET printed in red across the top. There was a pencil dangling from it on a string.

'Ernest's the name. I told you before. Write it down.'

'Cor!' Lucy breathed, as I took the pad and tried but couldn't make the letters work. 'He pulled it straight out of your head like a drawer. How did you do it, Ernest?'

Ernest's smile grew bigger. 'Like this!' pulling a long gold streamer from Budge's ear and tossing it high so it looped round the sparkly letters.

'Or this.' He put a hand between my neck and pyjama collar, bringing out two of the biggest cream doughnuts in the world. He gave us one each. Then leaned over the cot, taking a chocolate rabbit from Budge's bare toe.

Lucy's eyes got wider and wider. Ernest looked smug. 'How about this then?' He snapped his fingers.

It was as if someone had taken the weights off Lucy's feet. She floated up into the air, spread her arms and sailed round the room. Ernest looked at me.

'Want a go?'

I nodded.

He nodded . . . and there I was zooming past the picture rail, over the wardrobe, circling the light bulb, then swooping close to Budge's head as he sucked his rabbit and stared. It was smashing! Finally we landed.

'Oh Ernest, you *are* clever,' Lucy gasped.

'It's nothing,' he said modestly, but anyone could see he was chuffed to blazes. He drew a clock face on the floor and looked at the hands. 'Time's nearly up . . . but perhaps we've enough minutes left for one more trick. What'll it be?' and before anyone said anything: 'Right you are, Lucy!' pointing his umbrella at her dressing-gown pocket which began to bulge and wriggle. A black furry head popped up. Two big green eyes looked at us, then round the room. Before you could blink, a streak of black whizzed through the air and landed on the cot rail, missing the dinosaur by a hair. It fell upside down in Budge's cot. The kitten followed. There were hisses and squeaks, then howls from Budge.

Lucy yelled: 'It'll eat it!' She dashed for the cot, on the way accidentally hooking an arm through a streamer loop, then tripping up. I heard a tinkling crash like windows breaking, and saw the letters fall in a shattered heap. Budge howled louder still, and in the middle of the racket Dad appeared in the doorway, steamed up and ready to tell us off. But the words never happened. What did happen was Ernest whirling his umbrella, shouting:

'STOP!'

And we did. Like a film breaking down. Only Ernest could move. He drew back the curtains. Outside, hovering over our balcony, was a shadow. It was shaped like a garden broom, with an old-fashioned plane cockpit at the handle end, and inside it—I'm not sure, but it might've been a pointed hat.

'She's on time. Splendid!' Ernest said, and using his umbrella, did a neat pole vault, slotting himself feet first through the open window, like an envelope through a letter-box. I saw him disappear into the cockpit. Two hands waved. A fading voice called:

'GOOD . . by . . . e. . . .'

The moon went behind a cloud.

Sometimes when you wake up in bed in the mornings there are dream bits hanging about in your head. Nothing makes sense. It was like that, Boxing Day morning.

Lucy came into my room hugging a black kitten. 'Look what Mum's given me!'

I sat up. '*Mum?*'

She frowned, sort of puzzled. 'I . . . think . . . so.'

On the chair by my bed was an empty DON'T FORGET pad. A pencil too—on a string. I picked them up.

'*Wish* I knew,' I muttered.

'What?'

But I was watching sprawly purple letters writing themselves across the pad:

> *Wish right,*
> *Wish well,*
> *Yours ever,*
> *Ernest Spell.*

Lucy peered over my shoulder just as I was working out my second wish. 'Who's Ernest Spell?'

Quickly I stuffed the pad under my pillow. If she didn't know, I wasn't going to tell her.

From the kitchen Mum called to us: 'Breakfast. Move, you two! Dad's getting our bikes out. We've got a lot to do today.'

They'd worked! Both wishes had really worked. Good old Ernest. Now if we were going for a bike ride and someone had a puncture. . . .

I grinned at Lucy. 'Tell you later,' I said and started pulling on my jeans.

Grey goose and gander,
Waft your wings together,
And carry the king's fair daughter
Over the one-strand river.

BIRDS AND
BEASTS

Cuckoo Song

RUDYARD KIPLING

'Heffle' is Heathfield, a village in Sussex where a Cuckoo Fair is held every year on April 14. There is a legend that an old woman used to let the first cuckoo of the year out of her basket at 'Heffle Fair', and its echoing song as it flew away over Sussex meant that summer had come at last.

Tell it to the locked-up trees,
Cuckoo, bring your song here!
Warrant, Act and Summons please,
For Spring to pass along here!
Tell old Winter if he doubt,
Tell him squat and square-a!
   Old Woman
     Old Woman
       Old Woman's let the Cuckoo out
       At Heffle Cuckoo Fair-a!

March has searched and April tried—
'Tisn't long to May now,
Not so far to Whitsuntide
And Cuckoo's come to stay now!
Hear the valiant fellow shout
Down the orchard bare-a!
   Old Woman
     Old Woman
       Old Woman's let the Cuckoo out
       At Heffle Cuckoo Fair-a!

Cuckoo Fair

RUTH C. PAINE

One April evening, long ago, old Mother Merriweather stood in her cottage porch muttering and peering into the chilly green twilight. Her old brown hands, wrinkled and gnarled as the apple trees in her garden, wove wheedling, beckoning signs towards the darkening sky.

'Come on! Come *on*!' she murmured. 'You be late, m'dear! Where be you, m'liddle dear? Come! Come!'

At her feet lay a big market basket of brown eggs, yellow butter-pats and round white cheeses.

'There be jest room fer you, m'dear. Come! Come! Come!'

So, muttering and beckoning, she scanned the sky with her old eyes until at last she spied a tiny speck in the silver mists that lay above the dark forests of the Weald. The speck grew and grew, took bird shape, flew nearer and nearer, until it sank with softly fluttering wings into old Mother Merriweather's market basket.

She grinned toothlessly down at the small bird with dark silver bars on its white breast.

'So you be come, m'dear,' she crooned. 'And summer be come wi' you.'

She tied a snowy cloth over the basket, and left it in the porch when she hobbled up to bed. Tomorrow was April the fourteenth and she must be up at dawn to take the cuckoo to Heathfield Fair. There she would let him fly away and when the good folk of Sussex heard his song they would rejoice, knowing that summer had come.

'My bit o' magic!' she whispered happily as she pulled the bed covers up to her chin. 'My own lovely bit o' magic! Nubbudy but me can call the cuckoo, and nubbudy but me can let him fly. THEY gave the gift to old Mother Merriweather ages long agone . . . beyond the mists o' time . . . beyond the mists o' time.' Smiling, the old woman slept.

Now, in the cottage next door lived old Gaffer Winterthorne, a meddlesome, mischief-making old fellow who never could mind his own business. He was peeping from his kitchen window when old Mother Merriweather was making her good magic, and he chuckled nastily into his whiskers.

'Lot o' nonsense this be,' he scoffed. 'Why should her be in charge o' the cuckoo? Now, what can I do to upset things, hey?'

He sat thinking for a long time. He was still there at midnight when the painted wooden cuckoo in his clock on the wall popped out and called 'Cuckoo' twelve times.

Old Gaffer Winterthorne thumped the table. 'Ha! Got it!' he cried. 'I'll have a real live cuckoo in my clock instead of a toy one, and I'll make old Mother Merriweather look a proper cuckoo herself when she opens her basket at Cuckoo Fair.'

Thereupon he took the wooden cuckoo out of the clock and hurried with it round to his neighbour's porch. The stars winked reproachfully as he lifted a corner of the cloth and took from the basket the lovely living bird. Its feathers were soft and warm, and its tiny heart beat fast under his clumsy hand. He left the painted wooden cuckoo in the basket and hurried home. He chuckled to think what a very clever thing he had done as he popped the live bird into his clock and closed the tiny door.

'A *real* cuckoo clock I have, now,' he said. 'And how the folk will mock old Mother Merriweather come morn!'

Old Mother Merriweather was up betimes and off to the Fair, her basket on her arm. A chattering crowd quickly gathered.

'It's old Mother Merriweather—watch out children, and see the cuckoo fly!'

Old Mother Merriweather bent and whisked away the cloth. But no cuckoo flew joyfully upwards. Only a stupid wooden bird gazed up with painted eyes.

'Aw!' and 'Ooh!' and 'Aah!' sighed the people. 'Old Mother Merriweather has lost her magic powers!' Some laughed and pointed scornfully, but most wept because the cuckoo had not come, and there would be no summer that year.

Old Mother Merriweather stared down at the wooden cuckoo and she burst into tears. 'Oh my! Oh my!' she sobbed. 'Whatever can ha' happened?' But she soon understood and was very angry indeed.

'It's that old Gaffer Winterthorne,' she stormed to herself, 'I know him and his tricks.'

She unloaded her eggs and butter and cheeses on to the nearest stall, and taking up her basket she hurried home.

Breathless and red in the face she hobbled up old Gaffer Winterthorne's garden path and banged on his door. He opened his lattice window.

'Be you after summat?' he asked innocently.

'After summat?' the old woman raged. 'You know full

well what I'm after. What ha' you done wi' my cuckoo?'

The old man slammed his window shut.

Old Mother Merriweather stooped to the keyhole of his door and cried, 'If cuckoo don't fly, summer won't come!'

Old Gaffer Winterthorne did not answer.

'And if summer don't come your beans and peas and taters won't grow!' she added.

The old man began to doubt if he had been so very clever after all.

'And there'll be no flowers, and the bees won't make honey, and I'll tell everyone whose fault it is. They'll be after you, surelye, you see if they ain't!' old Mother Merriweather went on, kicking the door.

Old Gaffer Winterthorne kept silent, but he trembled a little.

Then the old woman screamed, 'If you got my cuckoo in your clock you're a proper daft old man, I reckon. He'll never call cuckoo while he be shut in a clock. He'll jest mope and die!'

Old Gaffer Winterthorne's jaw dropped open. Now that he came to think about it he realised the cuckoo had made no sound since he put it in the clock.

He jumped up and opened the little door. Sure enough, the poor bird sat with drooping wings and hooded eyes.

He snatched it from the clock, opened his front door, and thrust the dying bird at the old woman.

'Here, take your old cuckoo,' he said. 'He be nigh dead, I reckon, like you said. Give me my lovely painted wooden bird!'

Old Mother Merriweather flung the wooden cuckoo at him and seized her darling bird. She stroked its feathers and whispered words of love. She wove her good magic over it, and its wings began to flutter. Then she put it in her basket and hurried back to the Fair.

Once more the people gathered. Old Mother Merriweather beamed round at them. She stooped and whisked the cloth from her basket. Up flew the cuckoo, joyous and free, away into the blue. It sang, 'Cuckoo, cuckoo, cuckoo,' and the people cheered and threw their hats in the air, and all over Sussex they danced for joy that summer had come.

Cure for a Stye

JAMES WOODFORDE

An entry from the diary of a country parson, living in Norfolk nearly two hundred years ago:

March 11th, 1791 The Stiony on my right Eye-lid still swelled and inflamed very much. As it is commonly said that the Eye-lid being rubbed by the tail of a black Cat would do it much good if not entirely cure it, and having a black Cat, a little before dinner I made a trial of it, and very soon after dinner I found my Eye-lid much abated of the swelling and almost free from Pain. I cannot therefore but conclude it to be of the greatest service to a Stiony on the Eye-lid. Any other Cat's Tail may have the above effect in all probability—but I did my Eye-lid with my own black Tom Cat's Tail.

Witchcat Watchcat

RUTH McDONALD

Ebenezer was a watchcat. Ever since he had come to live with the McGregors, he had been in the habit of sitting by the front gate, watching. He knew every car in the street and most of the people as well. He knew which children rode bicycles and which children had roller-skates. He was friendly with the paper boy, the postman and the milkman. The dustmen waved to him when they collected the rubbish. Old people stopped to talk to him, mothers pointed him out to their toddlers and babies—even dogs sometimes came to say hallo.

But although Ebenezer was good at watching everyone in the street, he didn't scare people away as a barking, growling watchdog might have done. Instead he tried to encourage people in. He would roll on the path and wave his tail, miaowing and purring. Then he would get up and move towards the front door, running back to rub against people's legs and make them feel welcome. In fact, it almost seemed as though Ebenezer was watching out for someone special—waiting for someone.

Now, I haven't mentioned this before, but Ebenezer was very big and very black. He was also rather strange. He had this habit of catching mice, bringing them inside, and then letting them go. Mrs McGregor said she had never had so many mice in the house before. He once brought in a frog, and he often caught lizards. He also had a great affection for Mrs McGregor's broom. He liked to lean up against it and sleep close beside it.

No one knew where Ebenezer had come from. He had just arrived at the front door one day and miaowed until someone came to see what he wanted. Then he pushed his way inside and acted as if he belonged there. Once or twice Mrs McGregor had carried him out on to the footpath, but he had always run straight back inside. She had asked all her friends and neighbours if anyone had lost a black cat, but no one had. Ebenezer played so nicely with the children that she had decided he could stay. So every morning and evening he would sit by the front gate, watching. And that is just what he was doing one morning when Mrs McGregor and her daughter Miranda were making pancakes, and Miranda's little brother Jason was sitting on the floor licking a spoon.

'Bother,' said Mrs McGregor, 'there's no more sugar. I'll go next door and see if I can borrow some. Miranda—would you look after Jason?'

Miranda was pleased. She liked being left in charge. But as soon as Mrs McGregor was out of sight, down the street strolled a strange-looking woman with an old hat on her head and an old pack on her back. Ebenezer was sitting by the gate in his usual fashion, watching and waiting. When he saw the strange-looking woman he became very excited. He rubbed against her legs so hard that he almost knocked her over. He rolled on the path and purred and miaowed in such a way that of course she stopped to look at him, and of course he invited her in. Very soon she was standing at the front door ringing the bell.

Miranda had just put the first pancake into the pan,

and she didn't really want to stop and answer the door. But she went to see who was there, and when the door opened, in came Ebenezer with his tail held high. Behind him walked the strange-looking woman.

'Good morning, good morning,' she said. 'Are you the lady of the house?'

'Why, yes,' said Miranda, 'I suppose I am.'

'Then let me show you something,' the woman went on, taking a small green bottle out of her pack. 'I'm sure you'd like to try some.' But then she smelt the pancake cooking. 'Pancakes!' she said. 'I love pancakes. Watch this.'

Walking through to the kitchen, she picked up the pan and tossed the pancake high into the air. And although she only tossed it once or twice, there on the plate was a large pile of pancakes, freshly cooked and ready to eat.

'Now let me see . . .' she said, 'some sugar?'

'There's no sugar,' said Miranda. 'My mother . . .'

'Sugar!' said the stranger, and now there were three full bowls on the table—one with white sugar in it, one with brown and one with pink.

'Pink sugar!' exclaimed Miranda, but the stranger was once again holding out the green bottle.

'Just the thing to go with pancakes and sugar,' she said.

Ebenezer was looking anxious. The woman unscrewed the cap of the bottle.

'Try some,' she said. 'You'll feel better than you have ever felt before.'

'But I feel all right now,' protested Miranda.

Now, Ebenezer had a very special miaow which he kept for very special occasions. It was not his hungry miaow and it was not his welcoming miaow. It was the sort of miaow that is very hard to describe. But if you heard it you would certainly come running to see what was going on, because it was a loud miaow and a long miaow—a miaow that could make your hair stand on end and your heart begin to thump. And when he miaowed that very special miaow, his eyes became strangely bright, and his ears lay flat along his head. It seemed to him that now was the time to use his very special miaow. So he did.

Well! It was so loud and so long that Mrs McGregor could hear it next door, so of course she came running to see what was going on. And this is what she found.

Jason had stopped licking his spoon and was beginning to cry. Miranda was trying to clean up the mess—because after he had miaowed his very special miaow, Ebenezer had jumped on to the table, knocking over the small green bottle, and liquid was dripping down the table-leg on to the floor, and some had spilt on to Mrs McGregor's best pot plant.

'Whatever is happening here?' asked Mrs McGregor.

'Why, nothing!' said Miranda, '. . . at least, nothing very important.'

'It looks important to me,' said Mrs McGregor, picking Jason up and rocking him in her arms. 'What's that?'

She stared at the pancakes and the three bowls of sugar. She stared at her beautiful pot plant. And while she stared it started to grow. It grew bigger and brighter than ever before!

'Whatever is in that bottle?' she asked. 'And where's Ebenezer? I'm sure I heard his miaow.'

But Ebenezer had disappeared. So had the strange-looking visitor. And the odd thing was that Ebenezer did not come back.

But then he never had belonged to the McGregors. He was really somebody else's cat, you know!

Salamander

BENVENUTO CELLINI

Benvenuto Cellini was an Italian artist and goldsmith, who was born in Florence in 1500. This is from his own account of his life:

When I was about five years old, my father happened to be in a basement-chamber of our house, where they had been washing, and where a good fire of oak logs was still burning. He had a viol in his hand, and was playing and singing alone beside the fire. The weather was very cold. Happening to look into the fire, he espied in the middle of the most burning flames a little creature like a lizard, which was sporting in the core of the intensest coals. He had my sister and me called, and pointing it out to us children, gave me a great box on the ears, which caused me to cry with all my might. Then he pacified me by saying, 'My dear little boy, I am not striking you for anything that you have done, but only to make you remember that the lizard you see in the fire is a salamander, a creature which has never been seen before by any of whom we have credible information.' So saying, he gave me some pieces of money, and kissed me.

Cities drowned in olden time
Keep, they say, a magic chime
Rolling up from far below
When the moon-led waters flow.

So within me, ocean deep,
Lies a sunken world asleep.
Lest its bells forget to ring,
Memory! set the tide a-swing!

Against Oblivion

HENRY NEWBOLT

The Pirates and the Drowned Bells

ANNE ENGLISH

What I am going to tell you about happened when I was on holiday with my parents, travelling up the wild, west coast of Scotland. I was dead bored. There was nothing but scenery, and to make things worse my Mum went everywhere with this guidebook in her hand. It told you all about the coastline, and the ruins, and the history of every single place from the year dot.

But one place we visited, this ruined abbey, I'll never forget. It was up a glen, hidden from the sea by a bend in the fast-flowing river. Tall trees stretched their branches over the ruins, sheltering them from the sea breezes. It looked so calm and undisturbed.

'It says here,' said my Mum, eyes on her book as usual, 'that this used to be one of the grandest and wealthiest abbeys in the north.'

I sighed, but she went on reading. 'Over hundreds of years it amassed great wealth; gold and silver plate, and the finest of manuscripts. It became famous for its peal of bells, a gift from the people who lived in the glen. The monks ran a school here for boys—just about your age, Alan.'

I groaned. 'It's the holidays, Mum.'

'All right,' she said, 'I won't read any more. The next bit's just about the pirates anyway.'

'Pirates?' I said. 'What pirates? What happened? Tell me.'

But she'd already closed the book. The guide was collecting the visitors together to show them round the Abbey, and Mum and Dad went to join him. 'Are you coming?' Mum called back.

I said I'd sit there in the sun, and maybe have a look at her book. She seemed surprised, but she didn't say anything.

I watched, hands clasped round my knees, as they crossed the stretch of close-cut grass to the Abbey buildings. The walls were quite high in places, huge blocks of deep-red stone. At one corner were the blackened remains of a square tower, without a roof, and at the other, facing the sea, a high arched window-frame of stone.

As soon as the tour began I picked up the book and started to read.

'Everyone loved the sound of the Abbey bells, from the silvery chime of the smallest bell to the deep boom of the great bell. Their ringing marked the passing of each day, and the monks were always sad when the bells could not be rung because pirate ships had been sighted off the coast. The pirates robbed and plundered without mercy, but from the sea the Abbey was not visible, and so they did not know of its existence.

'The youngest scholar at the Abbey loved the bells so much that he dreamed about them every night, and prayed each day that the monks would allow him to ring them. But they never did. One hot, still afternoon he went into the empty bell-tower, meaning just to look. He put his hand lightly on the long bell-rope and stroked it—

then, thinking one peal would never be heard, gave it a single gentle pull. From the tower rang out one clear and silvery note. That was all—just one note.

'But out at sea lay a pirate ship. The pirates heard the clear call of the bell. They knew that where there was a bell there would be an abbey, and an abbey meant wealth. So they hove-to until dark, then silently slipped ashore, rowing upriver to the Abbey gate. With blood-curdling yells they beat against the gate, determined to break their way in.

'The sound spread terror inside the Abbey, monks and boys rushing from their beds. At the Abbot's bidding they carried away the Abbey treasures, escaping through a small hidden door into the glen. The Abbot was the last to leave, and as he reached the small door the pirates burst into the building, yelling and swearing, overturning stools and scattering candlesticks.

'Their yells turned to howls of rage when they found that everything of value had been removed. "We'll not leave empty-handed," shouted the pirate captain. "Take down the bells."

'As the pirates swarmed into the bell-tower, the Abbot turned back. In a voice like thunder he cried out, "No good will come to you, as long as the bells are with you. This is where they belong." Then, sad at heart, he escaped into the darkness.

'With a great clattering and clanging the bells were removed, and as they left the pirates set fire to the Abbey.

'Back on board ship they stored the bells in the hold and prepared to set sail, but although a strong wind filled the sails the ship made no headway. From the deck the pirates watched the Abbey burning, growing fearful as the crackling flames seemed to reach out towards them. Then, deep within the hold, the smallest bell began to ring, a sad, silvery chime that made the pirates shiver. One by one the other bells joined in, the mournful sound spreading in ripples across the water to where the Abbey was burning.

'Terrified and deafened, the pirates shouted that the bells were cursed, and they would throw them overboard. As the hatches were raised the bells started to roll forward, ringing louder and louder. The wind rose to a shriek, and the timbers of the ship began to creak and strain. Then, with an almighty roar, the ship split apart, and down, down, down went the bells, the pirates and all.

'It is said that the bells still lie there, just off the shore, sighing and restless, hoping that some day they will return to the Abbey.'

Closing the book, I looked up at the gaunt building with its fire-blackened stones, seeing in my mind the high tongues of flame leaping through it all those years ago. I could almost smell the smoke.

Then, walking towards me, came Mum and Dad, back from their tour round the Abbey. 'It's such a gorgeous day, I think we'll have our picnic here,' Mum said. She unpacked the sandwiches. 'Egg or ham?' she asked.

My legs were stiff and I got up, stretching. 'I'll just have a walk down to the sea, but I won't be long, so don't eat everything,' I told her.

The sea was surprisingly close; the bay a curved pool of calm, blue water. I walked down to the water's edge, crunching over pebbles and shells. A boy of about my own age was already standing there.

And then without warning everything changed. The sky and the sea turned grey; white-topped waves raced in long unbroken lines towards the shore. Below the sound of waves and water I heard a clear silvery chime, faint at first, then growing louder, until a deep boom shook the air. It was spooky. I moved closer to the boy.

The boy turned to me. 'You can hear the bells too,' he said.

I nodded. There was no mistaking the sound—it was just as the story said. Yet I couldn't speak about it when I went back for the picnic; in fact I haven't told anyone, until now.

* * *

In the old days, church bells were often given names of their own. Among the best-known in England are Great Tom of Oxford, Bell Harry of Canterbury, Old Kate of Lincoln and Big Ben of Westminster. This is an old English rhyme (translated from an even older Latin rhyme, three hundred years ago) about the powers of bells to drive away evil, and quieten storms:

> *Men's deaths I tell, by doleful knell*
> *Lightning and thunder, I break asunder*
> *On Sabbath all, to church I call*
>
> *The sleepy head, I raise from bed*
> *The winds so fierce, I do disperse*
> *Men's cruel rage, I do assuage*

Storm Children

PAULINE HILL

I'm not one to swank, but I reckon I'm pretty good at lots of things. Not sums and spelling and Scottish dancing (my legs go wrong in the twisty bits) . . . but, well, scrambling eggs for instance, and sewing the hem of my sister's dress when it comes undone (as it does most times she comes home after chasing in the field with the Baker kids, they always find the filthiest places to skip and slide in). What's more, I'm always first up the ropes in the gym, and I finish first with my paper-round, if old Mrs Hennessey doesn't pop out in her red dressing-gown for a yarn.

There's no end to the things I *can* do. Sometimes when I feel sulky, I'll hunt out the posh writing-pad Aunt Cynthia gave me for Christmas and my red felt-tip, the one that I keep for recording Riotous Events, and make a list of everything I *can* do, just to cheer myself up. Loads of things.

1. *I'm the only one on our street who's actually grown hollyhocks*
2. *And great big sunflowers so that I can feed Mrs Pankhurst's hens with the seeds, and Mrs Pankhurst sometimes gives me new-laid eggs, so that's a bonus*
3. *And I'm always the first to find snowdrops in the woods*
4. *And violets*
5. *And last autumn I made ten jars of blackberry jam from blackberries I picked in the woods*

6.   *And I brush my dog Shaggy's coat till it glistens like spun silk,
     and he won 1st prize at the Dog Show*
7.   *And some kids haven't even got dogs they can take for walks
     in the fields and go down to the market to buy biscuits for*

But there's one thing that always really frightened me.
More than ghosts. More than witches. More than little
green men from Outer Space. I didn't tell anyone about
it, because looking at me you wouldn't think I was
frightened of anything, ever. But I couldn't get through
a thunderstorm without shivering and trembling and
getting in a right old tizz. Once I even wet my pants, I
was so scared. But I kept the fear to myself mostly. It's
better not to tell folks what you're afraid of, they find out
soon enough.

It really was strange how I came to be cured of
thunderstorms. Part of it's to do with Mr Trenchard, my
history teacher. He's mad on old buildings, monuments,
old crumbly houses and spooky castles. Once he took our
class to peer at a Roman Wall, all broken away and
powdery with beetles crawling all over, I didn't think
much of it. My Dad builds much better walls. I could've
summoned up a faint glimmer of excitement if we'd
actually seen Roman soldiers building it, but when I
mentioned it to Mr Trenchard he seemed a bit put out.
'Don't be stupid, Tracey. Try to use the few brains you've
got, child!' Which was a bit off. I can't stand grown-ups
who call me 'child'.

We had to do one of those questionnaires about the
Roman Wall. I got all the answers from Peter Green. My
marks were quite high in that questionnaire, it certainly

surprised Mr Trenchard. But I did like the stories he told us about our town in wartime. My mum won't ever tell me about the War, she says it's better forgotten; but Mr Trenchard keeps bits of old planes in his garage, and lets kids polish them, and he'll sometimes give out Mars Bars too. He's got a photo of himself in RAF uniform when he was a pilot in the Battle of Britain, he looked quite handsome in those days. One September night in 1940 his squadron shot down an enemy plane over Devil's Finger, just a few miles away. The pilot baled out, over the woods, but his parachute got caught in the branches of a tree, and he was killed.

Well, this year, we had a half-day holiday in September because the vicar said we'd worked so hard bringing in the stuff for Harvest Festival (HP Sauce and conkers was what soppy Jenkins offered) and he wanted us to enjoy the warm weather before winter set in. Shaggy was waiting when I got home after school dinner—mince and salad, I ask you—and we set off towards the woods.

Lots of deep blue sky, bright golden sunshine on the stubble fields, and Shaggy belting off after imaginary rabbits in the hedgerows. I love walking. Shaggy likes walking too. I've never known a dog who doesn't. So we must have gone four or five miles, and I hardly noticed the candy-floss clouds slipping off the edge of the sky.

But, stealthily, grey shadows crept up. I felt a plop of warm rain on my arm. And then . . . CRACK! A heavy rumble. Fields lately friendly with sunshine became eerie, sinister. A flurry of wind lifted the leaves under the trees. Shaggy slunk close to me, tail between his legs, and licked my hand. 'It's all right, boy,' I comforted him, knowing that he was scared too. A dagger of lightning knifed across the sky. Thunder boomed overhead . . . rain cut down in solid sheets. Terror gripped me . . . sheer blind panic! I must get away . . . anywhere, away from it all. . . . Stumbling wildly, I ran on through the trees . . .

I came upon the farmhouse suddenly. *Acres Bottom Farm* it said on the gate. One minute it wasn't there . . . the next it was.

I knew Mum wouldn't approve of me going up to a strange house, but I was so scared that I peered in at the window, and saw a big farm kitchen, with a wide and welcoming log fire roaring up the chimney—in September—and children, four, five, six of them, dancing in the firelight. I banged on the door, the children came rushing to open it, and a moment later Shaggy and I were inside the warm kitchen. It smelt apple-sweet and spicy with cinnamon. Rosy-cheeked, smiling, chattering like magpies, the children danced and clapped their hands. 'You found us. We knew you would!' said the tallest boy. 'We've been waiting so long.' They grabbed both my hands and pulled me into their frantic dance. They barely heard the claps of thunder, but I could see flashes of lightning through the windows. 'Don't you *love* storms?' asked one little girl.

'No . . . no. I don't.'

'But you *must!*' she cried. 'They're beautiful!'

Another deafening clap of thunder. The children laughed and laughed, dancing more furiously, forcing me to join in . . . making me dance and squeal and fight back against the storm with yells and laughs and dancing, dancing, dancing.

I don't know how long the storm lasted. It was over too soon for me. The fear inside me suddenly snapped, and I'd never felt so wild and happy as I did that afternoon with the Storm Children.

It was well into evening, a calm and pastel sky after the fury. 'I must go now.'

'Promise to come again! Promise!'

'I will! I will!'

Mum had seen the gathering black clouds earlier, and had feared for me. She was on the afternoon shift at the clothing factory that week. When the storm broke she phoned Dad. He wasn't pleased. He was working nights, and hated being woken early, but Mum can be very persuasive. He uttered a few ripe words under his breath and went out looking for me. He hunted high and low, asked each soul he met . . . but returned home alone.

Mum panicked, of course, and he got the sharp end of her tongue. She'd come home early from the factory—she does fuss a lot. She rounded on him fiercely, demanding, 'Haven't you found her?' She always tosses her head haughtily when she's mad at Dad. Dad says it's her 'High Dudgeon' mood.

So when I'd said goodbye to the Storm kids in the warm house and promised to come back with some blackberry jam for them to taste, I ran home to find Mum in a High Dudgeon. 'Well!' she glared crossly when I came in. 'A fine dance you've led us, young lady!'

'Hallo, Mum.'

'Dad's been out looking for you! Where've you been, you naughty girl?'

'I sheltered in a house. When the storm came on. You know. . . .'

'Of course I know how frightened you get. I used to be just the same! Which house was it? I've told you not to go into strange houses . . . not to talk to strangers. . . .' She was white with anger. Dad says though she gets angry her heart's in the right place.

'Oh, Mum,' I said, and gave her a hug.

'Which house?' Her tone softened. 'Which house, Tracey?'

'A farmhouse up near Devil's Finger.'

She didn't reply immediately. Then she said, 'There's no farmhouse up at Devil's Finger.' She looked sharply at Dad. 'Is there, Tom?'

'Well . . .' He picked up Mum's warning look. 'No. No farmhouse. There *used* to be. . . .'

'You must know it,' I said. 'It's a farm called Acres Bottom. Funny name, isn't it? Mum . . . you all right?' She'd turned so pale that I thought she was going to faint.

'I feel . . . a bit giddy,' she said. 'You know how I get.'

After, when Mum had popped round next door to see Mrs Pankhurst, Dad said, 'Your Mum's always been nervy, love. Ever since I first knew her. She was only your age, then. She still gets frightened sometimes.'

'By thunderstorms?'

'She's better than she used to be. But she gets jumpy about all sorts of things.'

'That place. Acres Bottom. . . .'

'There used to be a farm by that name. Back in the War: 1940, it must have been—bombing every blessed

124

night. An enemy plane was shot down near Devil's Finger. It crashed on the farmhouse. Terrible disaster . . . all six kids killed in their beds.'

I gasped.

Dad went on, 'They say Acres Wood's haunted by the ghost of the German pilot. People reckon they've seen him on September evenings. All nonsense, of course, but you know how your Mum gets.'

When Mum came back from next door, everything seemed different. I had suddenly grown older. I knew two things. I would never again be afraid of thunderstorms. And I knew that when I was Mum's age, I should never be afraid of things that still frightened her.

Months later, Mum asked casually, though her hands were clenched as she spoke, 'That day of the thunderstorm, Tracey. When you were in the woods that evening . . . you didn't see anything . . .?'

I laughed gently. 'Oh, Mum,' I said. 'You've been listening to those silly stories about the ghost of the German pilot.'

'Well . . . ?'

'Of course not. That's all nonsense!'

But I never told her what I *had* seen, at Acres Bottom.

The Men of Black Tup

FRANK CHARLES

'Where the heck are we?'

Kev turned the map upside down to see if a different angle would help.

'I shouldn't waste your time with that,' said Derek, easing his heavy rucksack off his shoulders and dropping it to the damp ground. 'You'll never get your bearings in this mist. We'd do best to hang around until it lifts.'

Kev peered through the surrounding murk and pressed himself closer to the stone wall, seeking some shelter from the steady drizzle that was finding too many weak spots in his anorak.

They were lost in a close, grey wilderness. To their left and right, the dark bulk of the wall stretched a few yards before plunging from sight in the thick, rolling blanket. In front of them, within their limited field of vision, stood clusters of bluey-grey mounds. Some were sharp and craggy, marking the points where an ancient seam of rock had thrust its way above the surface of the fell. Others were softer and rounder—and emitting a fine light mist of their own into the surrounding air. One of these stirred. A bulging flinty eye beneath a fine curly horn briefly surveyed the miserable humans before its owner dipped its head to continue nibbling at the short, coarse moorland grass.

'Flipping sheep,' Derek grumbled. 'You'd think their rotten coats would shrink in this weather.'

'I don't understand it,' said Kev. 'It was a fine, clear day when we left the lads at Keld.'

The Club was moving camp further down the Dale to Grinton; but Derek and Kev had decided to hike it over the fells, rather than go along in the minibus.

'These Yorkshire Dales are well known for their sudden changes in weather,' said Derek.

'What—even in summer?'

'Especially in summer. And don't forget,' Derek continued, 'we are pretty high up, up here. Much higher than Keld. In fact we're in the clouds at the moment, chum.'

They stared sullenly at the bleak picture before them. A number of paths and sheep-tracks crossed the foreground, and any one of them could have been their route. They had best stay put.

'It's kind of eerie,' Derek whispered. 'This mist seems to deaden everything. Even sound.'

He paused. The silence was oppressive.

'I could do with a quick "baah" from one of them,' he added, nodding towards a group of rounded humps, 'just to relieve the monotony.'

Even as he spoke, the placid sheep leapt and scurried— and in a flash vanished. Leaving only the jagged rocks.

'Now what's got into those stupid things?' asked Derek, bewildered.

'Search me,' replied Kev. 'Can't tell with sheep. Perhaps they heard something.'

'But there's nothing to hear.'

'Or smelt something, then.'

'Do sheep smell? Like dogs, I mean?'

'How do I know?'

'Well you said . . .'

'Hush up!'

'What?'

'Hush I said,' Kev urged him. 'Listen!'

Derek listened; but his ears met only the uncanny silence.

'Did you hear it?' Kev asked.

'No, I didn't. . . . Hang on! Yes, there *is* something!'

Slowly they rose from their crouch under the wall and turned to look over the other side, straining their eyes into the swirling mist.

Then they both heard it. A sort of gurgle followed by a hoarse cackle. Then a pause. Then a murmur. Then another gurgle, mixing with another cackle. Until gradually they made out the sound of laughter and the reassuring rumble of voices.

Derek heaved a sigh of relief.

'We'll make Grinton yet,' he said.

As the voices grew louder, a patch of mist darkened, rolled into a shape, and gradually emerged from the gloom as the figures of two men.

Kev and Derek watched as they came on up the steep fellside towards them—rolling with the effort of their climb. Both men were wearing heavy capes across their shoulders and brown corduroy trousers that wrinkled across the tops of heavy steel-capped boots. Their faces, beneath thick cloth caps, were hidden because as they trudged up the slope and chatted cheerily to each other, they kept their heads bent, engrossed in the nimble antics of their fingers.

Kev felt a strange chill in the pit of his stomach. He

reached out towards Derek, to drag him back into the cover of the wall.

'Hold it . . .' he whispered.

But he was too late.

'Morning!' Derek shouted, waving.

By now, the first of the men had reached his wall and was climbing the rough stepping-stones built into its side. He froze at the top.

'Hey up!' he called in return. 'Here's a thing, Nat. Two lads behind wall. Is thee all right there, lad?'

'Fine thanks,' replied Derek. 'Just lost.'

'You wait there.'

With this, the man dropped from the wall and was followed by his companion. Together they strode towards the boys.

'By heck,' said the first man. 'What are you doing up here on a morning such as this? Should you not be working or summat?'

'We're walking from Keld to Grinton,' Derek explained. 'Or at least we were until this mist came down. Oh, I'm Derek and this is my mate, Kev.'

'You'll not be from these parts then?' said the second man slowly, fixing them with his piercing blue eyes, bright above a bushy black beard. His lips parted in a warm smile.

'We come from Lewisham,' said Kev, overcoming his initial fears because the men were obviously friendly. 'The other side of London.'

'Ah. The south is it?' said the first man, his ruddy face crinkled into a grin. 'I thought such funny names must have been dreamt up in strange parts. My name is John.

John Littlewood. And this is my little brother, Nat Littlewood.'

He chuckled and Nat winked at them—for although John was big, he was dwarfed by his brother Nat, who towered above them, his solid chest set between broad, muscular shoulders suggesting a man of unusual power. Yet there was a strange delicacy in the way his massive, hairy-backed hands were holding a piece of material between their thick fingers.

Derek and Kev laughed too as they took in his size.

Kev asked: 'Can you help us at all?'

'To find track for Grinton? Aye, that we can,' said John. 'If you'd care to walk along with us to Black Tup, we can show thee thy way from there.'

'Great. Thanks!'

The two boys struggled into their rucksacks and soon fell into step with the men as they continued their way up the rough track.

As they climbed, the mist thickened; but still they pressed on.

'You must know this route well,' observed Derek, 'to find it in this mist.'

'Aye, that we do,' said John. 'Why me an' Nat could find it with our eyes shut. Every day we treks to Black Tup—bar Sundays, that is, when all Black Tup men and their folk churches in Grinton.'

'Black Tup?' asked Kev. 'What's there then?'

'That's where Nat and I works. Black Tup Level. In t'mine.'

'*Mine*,' Kev gasped. 'I didn't know there was coal in the Dales.'

'Who said owt about coal,' Nat growled. 'Lead mine, lad. Lead. And the finest.'

'Aye,' John agreed, his eyes once more fixed on his prancing fingers. ''Tis said that Dales lead can be found on palace roofs 'tother side of world. We toil to keep the princes dry.'

'Is it much further?' panted Derek, feeling the straps of his rucksack digging into his shoulders.

'About another mile or so,' said John. 'If it weren't for mist you'd see chimney above fellside.'

'It's a fair way,' grumbled Derek. 'How far have you come?'

'From down Muker,' replied John.

'Muker!' Kev staggered in his walk. 'That's at least six miles from here at the bottom of the valley. That makes seven miles in all to your work. Don't they have any works transport like they have for my dad's factory?'

'Nay, lad. I told thee. Me an' Nat walks. We all walks.'

'Fourteen miles a day,' said Derek aghast. 'It must take you ages.'

'A fair while,' John agreed sadly. 'Times it seems we're forever walking this road. But we makes good use of it with talking and knitting.'

Kev and Derek glanced at his fingers—then stared at the big hands of Nat. Sure enough, these burly miners were knitting!

'Er—it must be—er—difficult walking and—er—knitting,' Kev mumbled awkwardly. 'Suppose you dropped the needles?'

'They're safe enough,' said John Littlewood. 'Look'ee.' He shifted his cape back off his shoulders to show a pair of long curved needles. They sprang from what looked like two curiously carved wooden handles—one fixed either side of his torso, about the level of his elbows. From a huge pocket in his waistcoat a line of wool curved towards the needles' tips where it had been worked into the cloth. He moved his hands away, leaving the needles protruding from the handles and the cloth dangling before him.

He chuckled. 'As tight as Tan Hill.'

'I thought only girls and women knitted,' said Derek.

Kev could have thumped him for his tactless remark; but the men showed no sign of offence.

'The womenfolk and the lasses knit, too,' John explained patiently. 'All folks that can, must knit. Money from the mining is not enough to feed a family by itself.'

'So you sell what you make,' observed Derek.

'Most things,' said John, 'for our wool is well thought of. The best sheeps is found here in Swale—though them over Wensley, with their curly coated beasts, may argue otherwise. And Swale has best knitters, too. Nat here is one o' the best of them all. He makes a fine cloth and 'tis said that Mr Burns—who buys off us—sells the hose that Nat makes to cover a dainty leg or two down in London. Show 'em, Nat.'

Slowly, Nat unhooked the needles from the wooden handles at his side, drew a ball of wool from his pocket, and passed them with the knitted cloth to Kev.

The cloth was smooth to Kev's touch, but intricately stitched to form a subtle pattern. It was hard to believe that such a giant of a man had created such fine, delicate work. It was easier to imagine him, stripped to the waist with his brawny body caked in sweat and dust, tearing lead-ore from a rock-face with each powerful swing of his pick.

'There we be—Black Tup at last,' said John merrily. 'And mist be lifting too.'

The ground began to slope and the boys found themselves looking down into a hollow in the fellside. To their left they could faintly see three stone buildings, the furthest from them crowned by a tall chimney that poked like a grey finger towards a dull orange orb in the sky above. The sun was struggling through the cloud.

'I don't see any shaft or lifting mechanism,' said Derek, puzzled.

'I told thee, lad,' said John, 'it be a level. Black Tup Level. We walks into mine. Look over yonder.'

He pointed to where a dark cavern opened into the slope, like the mouth of a small tunnel. He turned to face a track which wound behind the buildings.

'That's thy path,' he indicated. 'It's easy to follow. Take it till you come to a little gill. Follow that down and you'll soon see Swale and Reeth. Through Reeth and over Swale will bring you to Grinton.'

'Got it. Many, many thanks for your help,' said Kev.

'You're welcome,' said John. 'Safe journey to you, lads.'

With this and a slight nod from Nat, the two miners strode towards the mouth of the level. The first, larger figure disappeared inside. The second paused to wave before following his brother.

'Nice guys,' said Derek. 'But let's get going. With this mist clearing we should be able to make up lost time.'

'Hang on a sec!' Kev stopped him. 'I've still got this.'

He held up the needles with Nat's knitting and the ball of wool.

'Twit,' laughed Derek. 'We'd best leave it at one of the offices for when they come off shift.'

In silence they walked towards the buildings. For a place of industry it was strangely still. There was no sound, save the shrill cry of a distant curlew greeting the sun. They trod carefully. The ground was littered with rocks and odd pieces of rusting, twisted metal. One looked like the wheels and axle of a small railway truck.

Theirs was the only movement.

They stood before the brown-stained wooden door of the nearest stone building. Gingerly Kev pushed it—and it swung inwards with a harsh creak. They peered inside. The floor was littered with stones and debris, whilst in a far corner lay the skeleton of a long-dead sheep, its skull catching the orange glow of the sun above. The building had no roof.

On investigation they found the other buildings equally derelict. Kev moved towards the mouth of the level.

'Hey. You can't go in there,' Derek warned.

'Look, we must give this back. There's bound to be someone near the entrance who can keep it for Nat.'

With that he entered the small, black cavern.

Derek rushed after him; but stopped at the mouth of the mine.

'Don't go too far!'

There was no reply.

'Kev! Kev! Kev!'

Derek struggled with the panic welling within him.

'O.K., O.K.'

It was Kev, staggering back towards the light, a dazed look across his features.

'What's up, Kev?' asked Derek.

'You can't get too far in there,' Kev whispered hoarsely. 'It only goes about twenty yards—and then the whole thing's bricked up. From wall to wall. From floor to roof.'

They exchanged not a word as they strode down the fell under the blue sky and brilliant sun. They scarcely noticed the sparkling gills, plunging through the rocks to the silver ribbon of the Swale in the valley below. At Reeth, they walked across the green, ignorant of the tourists oohing-and-aahing from their cars at the pretty stone cottages; and pressed on through the village to the humped-back bridge that carried the road over the Swale to Grinton. There, the squat square tower stood stubby above the ancient church.

Kev would never know what force drew him to do it. But as he reached the churchyard gate, he opened it and passed inside. His right hand still clutched the wool and needles. Derek followed him, puzzled, as his footsteps took him around the church amongst the tombstones. Suddenly Kev stopped. Beneath the shade of a lime tree, in the wall of the churchyard, was set a simple stone plaque.

Kneeling before it, Kev carefully pushed aside the grass and wild flowers that were half-hiding it. He nodded. Derek crept up behind to peer over his shoulder. Together they read the few words that time, wind and rain had almost obliterated:

Sacred to the memory of
NATHAN and JOHN LITTLEWOOD
who gave their lives to save their fello . . .
in the tragedy at Black Tup Lev . .
25th July 18 . .

Kev stared in disbelief at the needles and fine woollen cloth. Then, very gently, he laid them down in the grass before the stone.

'It never made a fine leg in London, did it, Nat?' he whispered softly.

As they stood there watching, the cloth seemed to shrivel and melt, falling away from the needles and dissolving into the grass—as softly as the two figures had emerged from the mist on the fell above. Soon there was nothing left. Except two long, curved, rusty strips of metal.

They walked sadly out of the churchyard and headed towards the camp site. And as if by instinct, they made a silent, solemn pact. They must not tell the other lads.

Who would believe them anyway?

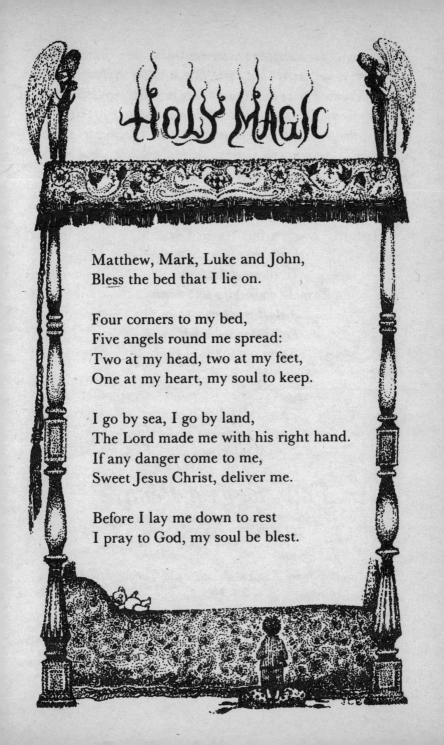

Holy Magic

Matthew, Mark, Luke and John,
Bless the bed that I lie on.

Four corners to my bed,
Five angels round me spread:
Two at my head, two at my feet,
One at my heart, my soul to keep.

I go by sea, I go by land,
The Lord made me with his right hand.
If any danger come to me,
Sweet Jesus Christ, deliver me.

Before I lay me down to rest
I pray to God, my soul be blest.

People used to put a staff in a dead man's hand, to help him on his last journey, and scatter herbs and flowers in the roadway as his body was carried to the churchyard. They gave him some coins, too, so that he could pay St Peter who keeps the gate of Heaven. These customs are very old—much older than Christianity itself. Thousands of years ago the Greeks would put a coin in a dead man's mouth to pay Charon, the ferryman who rowed the souls across the dark river which divided the world of the living from the world of the dead.

> Fresh strewings allow
> To my sepulchre now
> To make my lodging the sweeter,
> A staff or a wand
> Put then in my hand
> With a penny to pay to St Peter.

* * *

Four Eggs a Penny

RUTH L. TONGUE

This is a story from Rutland which Ruth Tongue first heard in 1908. Four farthings, or two halfpennies, made one penny.

Tom was very poor, and on market days he took eggs to sell. Sometimes there was only one, and he got a farthing for it. (If there were two, he'd leave one on the window-sill for the old beggarman who had nothing at all.) One day he was lucky; he found some nests, and he had twenty-four eggs to take, and that would be a silver sixpence for him. 'I'll buy a whole loaf,' said Tom. Then he thought of the old beggarman's egg. 'Oh well,' said Tom, 'I can get a piece of real bread for fivepence three farthings, and perhaps a bit of butter to go on it, and if he comes by when I come back, we'll have a feast, and he'll make me laugh.' So off he went to market, and there in the road outside the ale-house was the poor old beggarman lying dead.

Tom was very upset. 'He owed me a penny,' said the ale-wife, 'he can lie in the dirt for all I care.' Tom gave her four eggs, and four more for the halfpennies to put on his eyes for St Peter, then he went to the carpenter to make him a coffin, which was another four eggs. A farmer was kind, and took Tom and the dead man in his ox-cart to the parson, for nothing but thanks. 'The old man made me merry often,' he said, and Tom said so too. But the parson and the clerk, they wanted all the other eggs to bury the beggarman in a little dark corner of the churchyard on the north side. So Tom gave them his twelve eggs, and said a prayer for the old beggar, and came back home as hungry as he went. 'There's one potato,' he said. 'No bread or butter for me today. It'll be "Pull in my belt" and "Potato and Point".'

When he got in, there was a nice fire, and there on the table was a big loaf of bread, there was butter, and *twenty-four* eggs.

But there wasn't any egg on the window-sill.

Three Charms

The first two charms were written down by Robert Herrick, the vicar of Dean Prior in Devonshire from 1629 to 1674; the third is a traditional charm from Somerset.

Bring the holy crust of Bread,
Lay it underneath the head:
'Tis a certain charm to keep
Hags away, while children sleep.

* * *

If ye fear to be affrighted
When ye are by chance benighted,
In your pocket for a trust
Carry nothing but a crust:
For that holy piece of Bread
Charms the danger and the dread.

* * *

To preserve your cows against harm,
pour holy water down their throats
on Midsummer Day,
and sing the Creed to them
in Latin.

* * *

The Spunky

A spunky is the ghost of a child that died before it could be christened. It haunts damp marshy places (called 'zogs' in Somerset) in the hope that a passer-by will christen it with water and the sign of the cross, so that it can give up 'galleying' (frightening people) and join the happy dead who rest in peace.

The Spunky he went like a sad little flame,
    All, all alone.
All out on the zogs and a-down the lane,
    All, all alone.
A tinker came by that was full of ale,
And into the mud he went head over tail,
    All, all alone.

A crotchety Farmer came riding by,
    All, all alone.
He cursed him low and he cursed him high,
    All, all alone.
The spunky he up and he led him astray,
The pony were foundered until it were day,
    All, all alone.

There came an old Granny—she see the small Ghost,
    All, all alone.
'Yew poor liddle soul all a-cold, a-lost,
    All, all alone.

I'll give 'ee a criss-cross to save 'ee bide;
Be off to the Church and make merry inside,
   All, all alone.'

The Spunky he laughed, 'Here I'll galley no more!'
   All, all alone.
And off he did wiver and in at the door,
   All, all alone.
The souls they did sing for to end his pain,
There's no little Spunky a-down the lane,
   All, all alone.

The Girl Who Boxed an Angel

DOROTHY EDWARDS

Once upon a time a girl came from Jamaica with her family to settle in a big town in England.

Her Ma and Pa and her big brothers and sisters all got jobs; but this girl had to go to school. She wasn't old enough to go to work yet. And *did* she make a fuss!

'I don' wan'na go to school,' she said. 'What you wan'na make me go there for, every day? I don' like it.'

'You be a good girl,' her Ma told her. 'You just be a good girl. Mind your manners and work hard and you'll come out top in the end.'

'What's the good of that,' this girl said, 'when all the other kids are rough and rude and push me around?'

'You just say your prayers and ask the Lord to help you,' said this girl's Ma. 'Maybe he'll send an angel to

142

keep an eye on you if you ask hard enough.

'In the meantime,' her Ma said, 'I'll do a bit of asking on your behalf myself, and I'll write and get your Granpa to do the same.'

So that's how it was.

Now, one day this girl's class-teacher, who was soppy but nice, and called Miss Colley, read in the paper that the Insects Had Come Back. That after all the spraying of hedges with weed-killer, and the massacre of the proud wild flowers, and the death of the insects for whom the flowers grew, new flowers were springing up, immune to weed-killers, and more brightly coloured and strongly perfumed than their originals, and the insects had returned too and were brighter, bolder and livelier than ever!

'They are man's heritage,' said soppy Miss Colley. 'We must have a day in the country, children, and see them for ourselves.'

So Miss Colley with her 'C' stream and Mr Owen who took the 'D' stream arranged for a coach to take them all from the town to the far-off countryside.

Our girl from Jamaica (who was called Thomasina) was very glad to know Mr Owen was coming too, for while Miss Colley was too soft herself to notice any such unkindness as pinching or name-calling, Mr Owen was hard but just, and his small, dark, Welsh eyes missed nothing at all.

All the way in the coach the other kids mumbled sandwiches and spat pips, sloshed cola and started fights, so they hardly noticed the transition from town to country. Only Thomasina did that. She had nothing else to do, as

Fate had seated her beside Miss Colley on the side nearest the window, and as Miss Colley's attention was divided between the noisy C-streamers and Mr Owen across the gangway, whom she was said to fancy, Thomasina chose the window view rather than Miss Colley's back.

So she munched her bread and bananas and stared with wonder at the unfolding scenery.

'A green and pleasant land,' her Pa had called it in the days before they left the Island. Thomasina's Pa had been a soldier in the Second World War and had never forgotten the greenness and the pleasantness of the Surrey countryside where he had been stationed for his training spell. Thomasina, whose only experience of England so far had been dirty bricks and dusty trees, now looked out in awe and wonder at the lush growth and pleasant greenness, the moving sheep on the hillsides and the placid cows. Over the fumes from the engine came wafting the scents of meadowsweet and honeysuckle, and Thomasina sniffed loudly with extended nostrils like a little pony.

When they arrived at the selected spot the kids fell from the coach and began to rush about until Mr Owen blew a whistle-blast that brought them running.

'All right. Blowing off the old steam, is it?' said Mr Owen. 'Now I tell you what you can do and where you can go, right?'

Everyone nodded, and Miss Colley sighed in admiration. 'Oh Gadfan!' she said softly. 'How firm you are.'

'See: no further than that line of trees by the stream and NO ONE TO PUT SO MUCH AS A TOE IN THE WATER, MIND!' he bellowed. 'One toe and you'll be sent to stew in the old coach till it's time to go back, and a flea in your ear as well,' he warned them. 'It's Nature you're after today, not danger.'

'Just look at the insects,' bleated Miss Colley. 'Collect your specimens, and check your finds in the books. Ali, Paul, Yasmin and Jane will have the books. They will look things up for you.'

She began to hand out little plastic boxes with rings of muslin gauze set in their lids. 'Just one specimen each, children, and handle it with care. When we've all seen each other's finds, we must let them go free again.'

Mr Owen and Miss Colley settled themselves on a grassy knoll that commanded the view and the children scattered over the meadow, laughing as they ran.

The sun was now high in the sky and there were strange shimmers of heat on the distant roadway. All round the great meadow the hedgerows were rich with flowers so that they looked like over-blown gardens. Large caterpillars humped across great leaves, shining insects darted about the grasses, brilliant butterflies flapped lazily across the faces of delicious moon-daisies.

'No stupidities, mind,' shouted Mr Owen. 'Just look, and no larking.'

'One specimen each, remember,' trilled Miss Colley, who had taken off her little bolero jacket and whose creamy shoulders were gathering freckles as she sat.

Thomasina went slowly off after the others. It was real hot now. Down near the stream it was real, real, damply hot. Hotter than Back Home, because this was a different hotness. Clutching her specimen box she wandered drowsily along the lush grassy track towards the stream, where out-of-bounds dragonflies hovered over the water, showing off their blue-and-green spangles like suspended harlequins. The little stream had a life all its own. It pushed its way through rushes and jumped over stones, it played with leaves and harboured tiny fishes, and now and again it puckered small lips against the banks.

'Look out,' yelled Ahmed, pretending to push her.

'Boy!' thundered the Argus-eyed Mr Owen. 'Back up here where I can have my eye on you!' Ahmed trailed away to the middle of the field and began a feverish search in a tall clump of red sorrel.

Thomasina eased herself down onto the bank and stared at the dancing water and thought of Back Home, her Granpa who was a preacher, her Granma, her aunts and uncles and cousins, all together and gay and laughing—and maybe forgetting her already—under the bright skies of Home.

The stems of the beaked parsley teemed with insects. Rosebays swayed under the weight of enormous spiders who had spun a fog of cobweb mesh among their tropical-size pink blossoms. A dipper hopped from stone to stone across the glittering water, and a pair of trout in a deep hollow flicked their tails and muddied the stream about them. But Thomasina had clicked down the shutters of her mind and all she saw was the drifting breeze in the palm-fronds; all she heard were the shrill bird-sounds and the boom of the surf of Home. In her lap the plastic box lay forgotten. Thomasina, every pore open to the heat, drowsed in the tropical sun of Jamaica, and saw and knew nothing else.

'Look at that kid,' said Mr Owen. 'Just sitting.'

'Oh Gadfan,' whispered Miss Colley. 'Let her alone. She's happy, poor little thing. It's good to be happy, Gadfan.'

'There's soft you are, girl,' said Mr Owen, but he smiled and taking up a grass-stalk ran it along his sharp white teeth.

Thomasina saw her Granpa in his white tropical suit, with his bared head of white hair and his closed eyes, swaying a bit as he talked to the Lord. 'Just send an Angel to look after our little 'un: our young Thomasina,' he was saying. 'She don' like England, she sure fears them other kids. Oh Lord, send one little Angel to have charge of her.'

Li-Wong found a purple butterfly and Shamsha a squat, mother-o'-pearl beetle. Little Cheryl had a ladybird as big as her small finger-nail. Tobias brought an early chrysalis. The naughty Ahmed made peace with an offering of a yellow-spotted spider with diamond eyes. Mr Owen became quite merry and Miss Colley smiled, lazily happy.

Only Thomasina dreamed by the stream where the whispering grasses sounded like the breeze in the banana trees.

Suddenly Mr Owen got up and blew his whistle. 'All right, bring your boxes,' he shouted, and the children began to move in the direction of the little hillock where Miss Colley stood too, shaking the grass from her skirt, and patting her golden hair into place. The tardy ones opened their caskets to display their treasures, while Paul, Ali, Jane and Yasmin turned over the brightly-coloured pages of the Nature Books.

Thomasina's eyes, wide-open, saw nothing of this; the stream, the spiders, the dippers had all vanished long ago. Above her Granpa's white head the sky opened and a flock of baby angels came drifting down. Little floating heads with a fluff of wing behind them—like the gilt-framed, dark-glassed pictures on her Aunt Laurie's wall.

'Just one chee-rub, Lord,' prayed Granpa.

'Amen,' said all the folk. 'Amen to that.'

'Just one little Angel for our Thomasina in the U.K.'

Someone tapped her gently on the shoulder. Two anxious blue eyes stared into hers. 'Tommy,' a voice said, 'the whistle's gone. We've got to take our boxes up to Miss Colley.'

It was a little girl, Ashley. A fat little child who sometimes sucked her thumb when she was thinking. Someone so amiable she could even laugh at herself. 'Come on Tommy, collect something—before Mister notices.'

Thomasina got up and stared blankly around. The dragonflies still darted, but it would be impossible to catch them. The empty box lay at her feet. She stooped and picked it up.

'There's ants somewhere,' said Ashley anxiously. 'I'll look, shall I?'

Then suddenly a small breeze began to blow, small and light, rustling the leaves of the drooping willow-trees and feathering the grasses. It raised a pale strand of tow-coloured hair from Ashley's forehead and fingered Thomasina's black curls.

'Hey, look there,' cried Thomasina, her eyes wide, her mouth agape so that every tooth sparkled. 'Chee-rubs! Chee-rubs!'

Over the water, across the rushes, entangling in willows, drifting and sporting came a great cloud of small white fluffy specks. 'Chee-rubs,' said Thomasina. 'And just one little baby Angel for me to keep.'

As she spoke a fluffy speck detached itself from the drifting dance and landed on the front of her yellow dress. Carefully Thomasina raised her box, and opening the lid eased the small thing into it, closing the lid gently and lovingly over it afterwards.

'Come on, you lazy ones at the back there,' trumpeted Mr Owen through cupped hands. 'Let's see what you've collected.'

Boxes were opened, insects examined, checked and released. Surprised beetles, caterpillars, grubs and spiders were eased carefully into hedgerows or laid reluctantly upon flowers.

'You?' said Mr Owen. Ashley opened her box. 'A-h-h-h.' A green caterpillar tufted with black hairs flicked about with such energy that it jerked from the box, fell to the ground and vanished into the grass unclassified.

'And you?' said Mr Owen, putting out a bony finger to tap the lid of Thomasina's box.

'I've got a chee-rub,' she whispered, holding the lid firm shut. 'It's come all the way from my Granpa in Jamaica and I'm going to take it home.'

The ubiquitous Ahmed, who missed nothing, piped up. 'She's got a bit of fluff,' he said importantly. 'Some of that stuff that came from those plants round the back there. I saw her put it in.'

Thomasina stuck out her bottom lip. 'I want to take him home,' she said.

Mr Owen's dark brows began to bend in anger, but Miss Colley put in a quick word. 'Well, if it's only fluff, I don't see why you shouldn't,' she said. 'It's keeping insects that's cruel.'

At this unexpected sign of firmness in Miss Colley, Mr Owen looked surprised, but admiring too.

'You can borrow the box to take it home in, and let me have it back in the morning,' Miss Colley said kindly. 'And it's no good you saying it's not fair, Ahmed.'

'That's my lovely girl,' whispered Mr Owen, as they climbed aboard the coach.

'You sit by me this time,' said Ashley to Thomasina.

That night, alone in the bedroom that she shared with her big sisters, Thomasina opened her box and stared at the chee-rub. His little face was bright and merry, one gilt curl danced above his eyes.

'You can let me go now,' he said. 'You're O.K. You're going to be fine from now on.'

Thomasina believed him. Taking him carefully to the window she blew gently on his feathers and saw him sail off into the dusk.

A long time afterwards a clump of tall pink flowers struggled through the rubble of the broken buildings beyond the flat where Thomasina and her family lived. She passed them every day on her way to school with her shouting friends—one of a merry group. The flowers made her think of something, but she didn't quite know what.

Something she'd seen, or somewhere she'd been, perhaps?

'I'd like to pick some of those for Miss Colley to carry next Saturday when she marries Mr Owen,' she said suddenly.

'She wouldn't thank you,' said the practical Ahmed. 'They're only weeds!'

O, then, I see Queen Mab hath been with you.
She is the fairies' midwife, and she comes
In shape no bigger than an agate stone
On the forefinger of an alderman,
Drawn with a train of little atomies
Athwart men's noses as they lie asleep:
Her waggon-spokes made of long spinners' legs;
The cover, of the wings of grasshoppers;
The traces, of the smallest spider's web;
The collars, of the moonshine's watery beams;
Her whip, of cricket's bone; the lash, of film;
Her waggoner, a small grey-coated gnat,
Not half so big as a round little worm
Prick'd from the lazy finger of a maid.
Her chariot is an empty hazel nut,
Made by the joiner squirrel or old grub,
Time out of mind the fairies' coach-makers:
And in this state she gallops night by night.

from *Romeo and Juliet*
WILLIAM SHAKESPEARE

The Fairies

Come follow, follow me,
You fairy elves that be,
Which circle on the green,
Come follow Mab, your queen,
Hand in hand come dance around,
For this place is fairy ground.

When mortals are at rest
And snoring in their nest,
Unheard and unespied
Through keyholes do we glide,
Over tables, stools, and shelves,
We trip it with our fairy elves.

And if the house be foul
With platter, dish, and bowl,
Upstairs we nimbly creep,
And find the sluts asleep,
There we pinch their arms and thighs,
None escape, nor none espies.

But if the house be swept,
And from uncleanness kept,
We praise the household maid,
And duly she is paid,
For we use before we go
To drop sixpence in her shoe.

On tops of dewy grass
So nimbly do we pass,
The young and tender stalk
Ne'er bends when we do walk,
Yet in the morning may be seen
Where we the night before have been.

Half a Loaf Is Better
than No Bread

EDWARD THOMAS

True Thomas lay on Huntlie bank:
  A ferlie he spied wi' his e'e:
And there he saw a ladye bright,
  Come riding down by the Eildon Tree.

Her skirt was o' the grass-green silk,
  Her mantle o' the velvet fine:
At ilka tett o' her horse's mane
  Hung fifty siller bells and nine.

Thomas the Rhymer was in Fairyland seven years. As
he was lying one May-day on Huntly Bank he saw a
beautiful lady come riding towards him under the Eildon

Tree. So wonderful was her beauty that he knelt down in the fern before her, thinking she was Mary, the mother of Jesus. But she told him not to kneel to her. She was not Mary Queen of Heaven, but the Queen of Fairyland. She had come there to see him, because she had heard that he was a wise man who could foretell the future. Thomas looked at her again, at her face that was as bright as moss on snow, at her dress of grass-green silk and her jewels, and her horn of gold, and the falcon upon her wrist, at the silver bells hanging from the braids of her horse's mane, which was white, and at the hounds in the fern round about. She was so beautiful that he was willing to do anything she might ask. A second time he knelt to her, telling her he loved her and would go with her anywhere. She smiled and let him mount the horse behind her before she told him that if he came with her he would not be home again for seven years. Thomas had not lived so long that he could not spare seven years for the Queen of Fairyland; so together they rode away from Huntly Bank, day and night, through a land where they saw neither sun nor moon, but heard the sea roaring, until they came to a garden. From one of the apple-trees growing there the Queen plucked an apple for Thomas. 'This,' said she, 'is your wages. The man who eats this cannot lie.' 'Alas,' replied Thomas, 'that may be well in Fairyland; but what shall I do in the world if I cannot lie?' The Queen scolded him: 'Why should you think of the world when you have seven years of Fairyland before you? Would you lie to me? Did you lie when you said you loved me more than all women?' Thomas ate the apple, and put on the green cloth and the green shoes of Fairyland.

He has gotten a coat of the even cloth,
And a pair of shoes of velvet green;
And, till seven years were gane and past,
True Thomas on earth was never seen.

So much everyone knows; Thomas told it to all that asked him. But what happened in those seven years, why he came back to Scotland, whether he was glad to be back, no man pretends to know. Yet this one thing also has been told. All his friends had long given Thomas up for lost, except his mother. Every day she baked one of the small loaves that her son loved best, in case he should come home again. Every evening she cut the loaf in two to give half to a beggar; and next morning the other half went to Thomas's old dog.

Now, as chance would have it, Thomas returned at last on Midsummer Night; and this is the thing that is told of him after his home-coming. When his mother saw him she cried out, partly for joy, partly for sorrow that she had only half a loaf left. She hardly found time to kiss her son, so much was she troubled about the bread. Thomas comforted her as best he could, though he was True Thomas now, and could not lie. 'Mother,' he said, 'it's not for a man who has been seven years in Fairyland, and found his way home again, to complain about the bread; and in any case half a loaf is better than no bread.' After this he began to eat. Perhaps the bread took away his memory of Fairyland. Who knows? At least we know that True Thomas declared that half a loaf is better than no bread.

156

Goblins' Song

JAMES TELFER

O when the blushing moon
Glides down the western sky,
By streamers wing, we soon
Upon her top will lie:
Her highest horn we'll ride
An' quaff her yellow dew,
An' frae her shadowy side
The burnin' day we'll view.
 Ay lu lan, lan dil y'u.

A Fairy Ring

JOHN AUBREY

John Aubrey was born in 1626, in Wiltshire. As a boy he went to school at the little village of Yatton Keynell, near Chippenham:

In the year 1633–4, soon after I had entered into my grammar at the Latin School at Yatton Keynell, our curate Mr Hart was annoyed one night by these elves or fairies. Coming over the Downs, it being near dark, and approaching one of the fairy dances, as the common people call them in these parts, the green circles made by those sprites on the grass, he all at once saw an innumerable quantity of pigmies or very small people,

157

dancing round and round, and singing, and making all manner of small odd noises. He, being very greatly amazed, and yet not being able, as he says, to run away from them, being, as he supposes, kept there in a kind of enchantment, they no sooner perceive him but they surround him on all sides, and what betwixt fear and amazement, he fell down scarcely knowing what he did; and thereupon these little creatures pinched him all over, and made a sort of quick humming noise all the time; but at length they left him, and when the sun rose, he found himself exactly in the midst of one of these fairy dances. This relation I had from him myself, a few days after he was so tormented.

Joey Linny

MARY WEBB

It minds me of the tale of poor Joey Linny, poor soul. He was used to go wandering about, and once he come unbeknownst into a triple fairy-ring and they got him. Ah! they seyn it were like that in times gone. Folk burned witches then, and ducked 'em and dear knows what. And things was different. Any road, the fairies cotched poor Joey Linny, and away to go. But they seyn as now and agen at thrashing-time of an evening, when it's a bit wild and wet, you'll see a white, peaky face at the wind'y, with a bit of wispy hair flying in the wind, and it cries:

'Ninny, Ninny, poor Joey Linny!'

The Fairies' Farewell

RICHARD CORBET

Richard Corbet was born in 1582, in the time of Queen Elizabeth the First, whose elder sister, Queen Mary Tudor, was the last Catholic queen to rule England. When he was a boy many people still believed in fairies. But by the time he grew up and wrote this poem, King James was on the throne, the old beliefs were dying away, and fairies no longer played a part in people's everyday lives.

'Farewell, rewards and fairies,'
Good housewives now may say,
For now foul sluts in dairies
Do fare as well as they,
And though they sweep their hearths no less
Than maids were wont to do,
Yet who of late, for cleanliness,
Finds sixpence in her shoe?

Witness those rings and roundelays
Of theirs, which yet remain,
Were footed in Queen Mary's days
On many a grassy plain;
But since of late, Elizabeth,
And later, James, came in,
They never danced on any heath
As when the time had been.

WINTER IN THE WOOD

I fear that Puck is dead—it is so long
Since men last saw him—dead with all the rest
Of that sweet elfin crew that made their nest
In hollow nuts, where hazels sing their song.

'Tell me, thou hopping Robin, hast thou met
A little man, no bigger than thyself,
Whom they call Puck, where woodland bells are wet?
Tell me, thou Wood-mouse, hast thou seen an elf
Whom they call Puck, and is he seated yet,
Capped with a snail-shell, on his mushroom shelf?'

The Robin gave three hops, and chirped, and said:
'We found him lying covered up with snow
As we were hopping where the berries grow.
We think he died of cold. Ay, Puck is fled.'

And then the Wood-mouse said: 'We made the Mole
Dig him a little grave beneath the moss,
And four big Dormice placed him in the hole.
The Squirrel made with sticks a little cross.
Puck was a Christian elf, and had a soul,
And all we velvet jackets mourn his loss.'

EUGENE LEE HAMILTON